The Dead Woman in His Room

Revenge strikes from a forgotten past

By Mark Kindley

Copyright

Copyright @ 2023 by Mark Kindley

All rights reserved. No part of this book may be used or reproduced in any form whatsoever without written permission except in the case of brief quotations in critical articles or reviews.

This book is a work of fiction. Names, characters, businesses, organizations, places, events, and incidents either are the product of the author's imagination or are used fictitiously. Any resemblance to actual persons, living or dead, events, or locales is entirely coincidental.

Printed in the United States of America.

For more information:
    Email: mark@kindley.com
    Website: https://www.kindley.com

Dedication

I want to thank my wife Carol and my daughter Tosha for being in my life and providing me countless reminders that we are never in control of the decisions and experiences of the people we care most about. Life is a much wilder ride than that.

I want to thank my friends Steve, Tim and Merrill for their willingness to be first readers of my novel, and my friend and colleague Arthur for his invaluable help and encouragement in formatting my book for publication.

In a broader sense, I owe gratitude to the countless characters in my checkered past who opened my eyes to the swirling, interconnected mysteries of life.

I also want to thank readers who have been willing to take a chance on this book and to welcome them to the fictional world of Mill River. None of the places or people in this novel are real…except in this book.

Take care. Stay well. Enjoy.

Mark

Contents

1 "How's your father?" — 1
2 "Not funny. Call me." — 5
3 "Please don't tell him I was here." — 11
4 "Why are you doing this to me?" — 14
5 "I know about HAL Holdings." — 21
6 "She was here when I got here." — 31
7 "So, what do you want from me?" — 41
8 "And take those beaner kids with you!" — 49
9 "Anything you haven't done yet, Bud? — 60
10 "Everyone choose a buddy." — 73
11 "How long has she been gone?" — 83
12 "Not your fault, man. Not your fault." — 93
13 "Get in!" — 107
14 "I wish I had died before this night." — 118
15 "The police are coming!" — 127
16 "Don't let anything else happen before I get there." — 141
17 "Can't talk. He's here!" — 151
18 "I've got your bitch!" — 157
19 "I killed them with a knife so I could watch them die." — 170
20 "We're family." — 177
About the author — 182
Books by the author — 183

1

"How's your father?"

Nick, Jr. resists the temptation to take a shortcut across the broad lawn to the front door of the restored Victorian house in Sausalito where Kyle Leary lives. It has taken him three years to find Leary, and it takes all his self-control not to rush ahead when he is this close to finally confronting him. Kyle Leary isn't Kyle Leary anymore. He's Shamus Bourne, a rich art collector who lives on a hill that overlooks the bay. The fake name delayed this moment, but it wouldn't change the outcome. Nick, Jr. would have his due.

Nick resents every good thing that happened to Kyle in the more than 25 years since he helped Nick's father steal what should have belonged to him and his mother and sister. The beautiful view, the perfect lawn, the manicured shrubbery, the flagstone walkway; every aspect of this house makes him angry, and his anger increases with every step he takes toward the front door. He isn't usually angry when he goes to kill someone. Most of the people he's paid to kill he doesn't know. This one he is doing on his own.

Kyle is standing at the window of his office on the second floor looking out at the slanting rays of the sun through the afternoon clouds. He loves the light at this time of day. He feels detached from the scene below him and doesn't pay much attention when he sees Nick's car pull into his driveway. Probably some Mormon missionary, he thinks; although they usually came on foot, and in pairs. Very few cars pull through the gates into his driveway. He isn't expecting anyone, and he has no intention of talking to strangers on his doorstep. He is alone, as usual, but the house is very secure.

It irritates him that this person has intruded on his reflections, and his irritation forces him to look at the man in the dark suit who is proceeding slowly up the walkway to his front door. He looks oddly familiar. He looks like a guy he knew a long time ago in Denver. He looks like Nick Barons. But he couldn't be. Candice told him Nick was found dead at his ranch above Boulder shortly after they folded HAL Holdings and disappeared from Colorado. The unwitting bagman was left holding the bag. The guy was a creep, anyway; a sleazy lawyer who thought he was a player. It couldn't be Nick Barons. He'd be old, Kyle thought. Kyle didn't think of himself as old, but he thought Nick would be old after all these years.

Whatever reluctance he has to meet this stranger is overcome by curiosity. Kyle isn't that curious about anything anymore. But this is curious. He turns away from the window, stops by his desk momentarily and then starts down the stairs.

They arrive at the front door at the same time. When Kyle opens the door, he flashes on memories of Bronco games and power lunches on 17th Street in Denver. Nick, Jr. is about the same age his father was when Kyle knew him in Denver. Nick grew through a stage when he looked like his mother's family. Now, in his 40's, he looks very like his father.

"Are you Kyle Leary?" Nick, Jr. asks.

"Who wants to know?"

Nick had thought about this moment every day for three years. He very much wants this guy to know who he is. He wants to see how he will react. "I am Nick Baron's son," Nick, Jr. says. "We need to talk."

Kyle opens the door and steps back to let Nick come inside. He isn't afraid. Kyle had played Nick Barons like a marionette, and he is sure he can do the same with his son. That's what Kyle did with people.

The floor in the entryway is polished marble. Kyle is standing at the base of a broad staircase with dark mahogany banisters. Light comes down behind him from a window on the landing. It's picturesque. In his silk shirt and linen slacks, so is he. Nick Jr. stands just inside the door. Now he's in Kyle's space.

"How's your father?" Kyle asks, with a disingenuous smile.

The question blindsides Nick. His father has been dead for 25 years. This guy has to know that. He isn't prepared for Kyle's question. Usually, Nick doesn't have to talk to the people he kills. He just kills them. He can usually control his anger better.

Nick looks at Kyle without saying anything. Then he closes the door behind his back with his heel and, in one motion, pulls a knife out and shoves its blade just under Kyle's ribs, yanking it back hard into his heart. Kyle looks at him with an amazed expression on his face before he drops to the floor. He is already dead. He never had a chance to outsmart Nick, Jr. the way he did his father.

Nick wipes the blade on Kyle's silk shirt as he retrieves the knife. There wasn't much blood. All the real damage was done on the inside. Then he looks down at Kyle lying on the polished floor. He feels nothing. He didn't enjoy killing Kyle as much as he thought he would during the three years he spent finding him. In fact, he's angry with himself now. He needs information. The killing was supposed to come later. Now he would have to search for the information he wants on his own, and he has no way of knowing how much time he has for his search. Or where to begin. He starts upstairs.

The Dead Woman in His Room

Nick enters an office on the second floor, and, on a broad mahogany claw-foot desk, he finds a laptop computer. It's in sleep mode. The laptop might be enough. Nick learned to work on computers in one of his stints in the penitentiary. It's been a very useful skill. It's amazing what people are willing to store on a personal laptop: access codes, passwords, email, proprietary information of all sorts. Nick always takes the laptop when he does a job.

Before he shuts down Kyle's laptop, Nick opens the "sent messages" folder. The last message Kyle sent was emailed to an AOL account. It's just one word, actually an acronym. In the subject line it says "HAL" in big letters. The message has no other content.

On his way out, Nick looks down at Kyle's body and sees his cell phone on his belt. He picks it up and puts it in his pocket. Caller ID is a wonderful thing. Why people think their cell phones are secure is beyond him.

"Stupid! The whole fucking world is stupid."

He shuts the door.

2

"Not funny. Call me."

Kyle Leary and Candice Bergeron haven't communicated much over the years. When they left Denver in 1978 there was a strong sense that the episode they shared was over. They moved on. At Candice's insistence, they did maintain a communication link that would be triggered if something happened to either of them that would indicate the perimeter of secrecy around HAL Holdings had been penetrated.

They participated in no other scams like that one either together or separately. After Denver, they lost the heart for it. They didn't need the money. Kyle changed his name to Shamus Bourne, and Candice changed hers to Constance DeBreaux. They both turned their backs on that chapter of their lives.

Candice happens to be at her computer in her home in New Orleans when Kyle sends the email message. There hasn't been anything except spam in that AOL account for years. Usually, she just scans the subject lines and deletes everything. Sometimes she just deletes everything without looking. This afternoon the three letters: HAL stand out like a brand.

On an impulse, she calls Kyle's cell phone. He doesn't answer so she leaves a curt message: "Got your email. Not funny. Call me."

Kyle was already dead.

The Dead Woman in His Room

The email sets off a cascade of memories and emotions from their time in Denver 25 years ago. It irks her that Kyle sent the message, which she assumes was some kind of prank. He never took security seriously enough. She did kind of look forward to talking to him, though.

In all the years since they left Denver in 1978 no one ever appeared on the trail of HAL Holdings. The scam was very good, she had to admit. It was the height of the Denver oil boom, and a group of exceedingly self-impressed, supposedly legitimate businessmen were so eager to hide money from their partners and families, as well as the IRS, that not one of them questioned that a private bank named HAL Holdings existed in the Cayman Islands. Their need to believe was stronger than their need to know. It did not detract from the scam that the men who pushed their money at HAL all reminded Candice of her adoptive father, with his pin-striped suits, his fancy cufflinks, and his little white fists.

The one problem Candice had with the way HAL Holdings went down was Kyle's insistence on involving Willie in the deal. Willie Lyons was Kyle's friend from New York. He was a jazz musician, a tenor sax player, who had stayed with Kyle and Candice in Denver for a few months between gigs. There was no need to involve Willie in HAL. Kyle was just showing off.

Candice knew that Kyle was in love with Willie, although Willie didn't know it. It was less apparent that Candice was in love with Willie, too. Not a romantic kind of love with illusions of running off and living happily ever after together. Willie didn't thrill Candice in her secret heart; actually, he made her uncomfortable. The men in her life—starting with her adoptive father—had all been sniggering, deceitful cowards who treated her as if they had some right to crawl between her legs whenever they felt like it. Willie was an exception. The gene that carried the expectation of superiority had apparently not been part of his DNA, and the deficiency wasn't fixed in his upbringing. He was the first essentially honest person she had ever met. Maybe the only one.

Candice could understand how Kyle could be in love with Willie, but she never forgave him for involving Willie in HAL. Willie believed Kyle implicitly, and Kyle had used his friend's trust to make Willie an unwitting poster boy for depositors in HAL Holdings. Not everyone believed Kyle, but everyone believed Willie. Candice took some moral satisfaction in deceiving Nick Barons and his ilk, but deceiving Willie was different. It made her feel cheap. From the day he left Denver, Candice distanced Willie from HAL Holdings as much as possible.

~~~

When Kyle doesn't call her back a day after she left the message on his cell phone, Candice begins to wonder if maybe his email wasn't a prank. Sitting at her desk, late that morning, she does a search on Google for "Shamus Bourne." Her search brings up a short story in *The San Francisco Chronicle*:

> SAUSALITO: Shamus Bourne, a wealthy art collector from Sausalito, was found dead in his home of a single stab wound to his heart. The house did not appear to have been robbed. The police are investigating, but there are no suspects at this time.

She reads it several times; taking in a little more of the implications every time. She feels shock. She feels anger. She feels sad. Then she feels undone. The call she made to Kyle on his cell phone. She realizes that one call could lead whoever killed Kyle directly to her. She feels a crumbling inside, as if she'd been turned to sand and it was starting to rain. She has to warn Willie. Using her alias, Constance DeBreaux, she books the first flight she can find from New Orleans to Bradley Field in CT. Then she shuts down her laptop, sticks it in her briefcase, and leaves immediately.

The Dead Woman in His Room

~~~

Nick follows her cab to the airport. He wanted to confront her in her house, and this time he was determined he would not be so quick to kill. Now he has to follow her and wait for the right opportunity. But he's good at that. He has uncanny patience when he is in pursuit of someone.

This time he'll get the information he needs. He knows his father put $2.3 million in a private fund called HAL Holdings. He assumes it's still there. His father was found dead only a week after making his last deposit. He also knows he needs to find out where the money is now and how to access it. There would be a code, maybe a series of codes. There's no way to break into a secure account without a code. He knows that. He would have to get that code from this woman. Then he would kill her.

~~~

Candice's plane arrives at the airport in Connecticut in the early evening. She rents a car and sets off immediately on the hour-and-a-half drive from Bradley Field, northwest of Hartford to Mill River. On the way there, her mind races back to Denver searching frantically through her memories for some clue as to who could have possibly picked up the trail to HAL Holdings after so many years. Some of those guys had to be dead. She tracked all the depositors for ten years, just to know where they were. It was with a certain amount of disappointment that she was forced to admit that losing money to HAL Holdings had not seemed to change any of them for the better; or even for the worse. As far as she could tell, they just continued on.

None of the money deposited in HAL was supposed to exist, so none of the depositors ever reported it missing. After the boom, they went back to what they had been before. Several were still in the oil business, some sold real estate. Some were lawyers. Some were brokers. Some just disappeared.

The Dead Woman in His Room

They were all sleazy, middle aged white guys who were willing to take advantage wherever they found it, but they weren't criminals, per se. It was impossible to imagine any one of them as a killer. This had to be someone else.

A hundred yards and one forest green SUV behind Candice, Nick is trying to think through who this woman could be and where she could be going. He is still so angry with himself for killing Kyle Leary before he got the information he needs, that he keeps squeezing the steering wheel as he drives and cursing under his breath. He found nothing useful in Kyle's laptop; nothing except the contact information for the last person who called his cell phone: Constance DeBreaux. Who the hell is she?

It's dusk, and there is a light rain. Nick can see the money his father stole from him receding from view—taillights in the increasing darkness on the winding, rainy roads of western Massachusetts. It makes him furious that he could blow this. This woman has to know. She is the one who called Kyle. She has to be the one who got the HAL email. She has to be involved. She has to.

She's about the same age as his mother would be if she weren't dead. Years of listening to his mother whining and getting fat and drunk and drugged up had all but extinguished any feelings that he had for her years ago. Still, he was taken by the fact that this woman in the car two cars ahead of him was the exact image of the woman his mother had wanted to be: rich, sophisticated, smart, and still beautiful. His mother had died stupid and ugly. She weighed seventy pounds more than he did. She'd lost a foot and then a leg to diabetes and was bedridden for her last three years. He couldn't even stay in the room with her. It stunk. And she just whined and whined and whined. God, he hated that whining. He hears it in the tires on the wet roads and it causes images of his mother to flash before him as he drives on staring through the car ahead of him at the taillights of the car driven by the woman who, in his fury, is becoming the image not just of the woman his mother wanted to be, but of all the rich, sophisticated, beautiful white women who were always beyond his reach because he was Mexican, or worse: half Mexican.

He realizes he's tailgating the SUV ahead of him and knows he has to calm down. Anger makes you obvious. He couldn't be obvious. He forces himself in his mind to go back to South Wind in the foothills of the Rocky Mountains where, as a child, he had first taught himself to sit quietly for hours, without impatience. He was homeschooled by his mother. He had no friends, but he had jack rabbits and snakes and coyotes and strange beetles and sage and hot sun. He wasn't angry then; he wasn't scared. That was before the divorce, before he was dumped in the barrio with his mother and sister. Hiding was a kind of meditation for him then, as close to peace as he ever found. Years later he learned to use that feeling when he was pursuing someone as a contract killer. In a way, the sense of peace that he got from hiding had become associated, in fact, with the killing. It was what made him very good at what he did. Anybody could kill out of anger.

There is no peace associated with killing Kyle. That was stupid. Nick Jr. is having a hard time finding calm and being able to focus. He's angry almost all the time now.

3

"Please don't tell him I was here."

Candice drives directly to the High Rise Apartments. She has never been to Willie's apartment, but she knows where it is. The High Rise was built in the mid 1970's when a craze for Bauhaus architecture swept through local school and town boards and resulted in a generation of angular schools and civic buildings that looked like geometric shapes arbitrarily stuck together. From a distance, the High Rise Apartments look like a container for some huge, odd-shaped appliance. At 12 stories, it is the tallest building in a town that consists mostly of sway-backed brick factories—many with their windows boarded up—and multi-family houses with drooping porches.

    That the building is so unlike anything else in town adds to the sense that the people who live there are in their own separate dimension, removed by a degree of familiarity from everyone else. People who live in the High Rise are called "High Risers" by the locals. It is a place apart. Although it was originally built as subsidized housing for the elderly, the state subsequently elected to place recovering alcoholics and drug addicts in the High Rise with them. The two types of residents are not compatible. When the High Rise was a community of elders, the residents felt secure. They left their doors unlocked and moved freely around the hallways and common areas. By introducing a troubled younger population into their isolation, the state took away their sense of security. The old people became afraid.

Murph, the head security guard, stops Candice on the way in. When she says she's a friend of Willie Lyons and needs to see him as soon as possible, Murph tells her that Willie is out with his nephew Pete. "They're usually back by now," he adds. "Pete has a room in the River Street Hotel. You might find them over there."

"Any message for Willie?" Murph asks as Candice turns to leave.

"No. I don't think so." She pauses for a moment. "Please don't tell him I was here. It's kind of a surprise. I don't want him to suspect anything."

"Okay lady. Up to you." It isn't anything he would say out loud, but Murph enjoys the thought that a woman like this one could surprise him anytime she wanted. She's not young, but she is very attractive. He looks down at his console of security cameras as Candice hurries away, but he looks up in time to watch her walk out through the front doors.

Nick watches her from the other side.

Candice sits for a while in her car. She isn't sure what to do. She feels that she has to warn Willie, but now that she's here, she isn't sure how to go about warning him. She isn't even sure what she should warn him about. She doesn't know who killed Kyle. It could have been a robber. That Kyle emailed her the three letters HAL right before his death, however, is too much of a coincidence to ignore. If this is about HAL, then it could involve Willie.

Candice is aware of Willie's condition. She knows why he is here. She isn't sure how much he can understand about any of this, at this point. She only spoke with him on one occasion after their night together in New York City five years ago when he told her about his diagnosis. It was just before he moved into the High Rise. She called him and offered to care for him. He could live with her; wherever he wanted. Anywhere in the world.

The Dead Woman in His Room

"No. I don't want that." Willie was adamant. "I don't want the long farewell. And you don't, either. That's not who we were, and I don't want that to become who we are. Please accept that. It will be easier for both of us. I'm okay here. Just let me go." He paused and took a breath. Before Candice could respond, he said, "I have to go now. Take care." And he hung up. This had been one of his good days.

Candice didn't call him again, but she was aware of him. She knew when he moved into the High Rise. She knew what kind of place it was, and she asked around enough to know that Willie was at least reasonably safe. She flew up from New Orleans to see for herself. That was the other time she sat in her car in the parking lot at the High Rise and didn't know what to do. She just sat there. She felt sad. She felt stupid. She felt like a 16-year old girl completely unstrung by some romantic idiocy. She had never felt that way before.

"I am 65 years old, for Christ's sake. What am I doing?"

She hadn't been back. Until now.

This is the first time she heard that Willie's nephew Pete is looking after him. She knew about Pete, but she never paid much attention to him. She knew he was a writer. Pete was Willie's sister's only child. Candice managed a trust fund for him that Willie had asked her to set up when Pete's parents were killed in a car accident. It was a blind trust, so Pete didn't know about her or even how much money was actually there. That had never been an issue. Pete never came close to reaching the withdrawal limits she had placed on the account. Maybe he was a little like Willie, she thought. No one in the family knew how to spend money.

Candice had honored Willie's request not to get involved in his life, but this time she feels she has to. She decides she'll have to trust this Pete. She doesn't know what else to do.

4

"Why are you doing this to me?"

Pete and his uncle Willie are having dinner at a little Portuguese restaurant that Pete found in his constant wanderings a couple of small towns north of Mill River. Riding in Pete's van is the one activity that consistently calms Willie when he becomes agitated. They'd been taking a lot of rides in the evenings lately.

Evenings are often difficult times for elderly people with Alzheimer's and other forms of dementia. Dementia patients so often become agitated and restless in the evenings that caregivers in nursing homes call the behavior pattern "sundowning." Sundowning is obviously a very difficult time for the person with dementia. It is also a very difficult time for the caregiver.

As a caregiver, Pete is flying by the seat of his pants. He reads everything he can get his hands on, but he is still operating mostly on good intentions and little else. His good intentions do not prepare him for the emotional and physical demands that caring for Willie are starting to make on him. Already tall and thin, he is losing weight. The two vertical lines on his face that appear like ripples behind his smile seem a little deeper. And it isn't because he's smiling more. He's 53 and his hair is thinning and turning grey. Never concerned too much about his appearance, Pete's hair is a little longer and little wilder than usual. It sticks out around the edges of the caps he likes to wear and makes him seem distracted. He looks like a professor in blue jeans and denim shirts.

Pete loves his uncle, or at least he loves the image he has of his uncle whom he only saw infrequently over the years. The image he has of his uncle is of an extremely talented, intelligent, and caring person who shared his gifts freely through his music and his enthusiasm for life. Part of Willie's success as a performer was his ability to make everyone in his audience feel as if he were playing just for him or her. His playing made people feel special. Willie was considered a musician's musician because he listened to the other players and played with them instead of over them. He made them sound good. He played solos with deep personal feeling, but, as he had often said, "The solo isn't the song. It's just part of the song." It was interaction with other musicians that drove Willie, not the limelight.

This image of Willie stands in sharp and sad contrast to the petulant, self-centered, bull-headed old man that Willie can become around sunset. It doesn't always happen. Usually, Willie seems to be carried forward on his charm and good graces even as his dementia progresses. At other times, he can act very convincingly like a spoiled four-year old in the throes of a temper tantrum. He sets his upper lip in a way that Pete has come to recognize as a sign of a difficult episode ahead.

It wasn't that often, but it was often enough to leave Pete with a vague sense of anxiety after dinnertime. Pete takes responsibility for all of Willie's meals at this point, either cooking them himself, going out or having something delivered. They have pizza or Chinese often. Pete isn't much of a cook. He isn't interested enough in food.

Pete is on the slippery slope that so many well-intentioned people find themselves on when they start caring for a family member whose cognition is deteriorating. There aren't many good options for long-term care and the person who is typically most steadfast against any of them is the very person who needs them. So, family caregivers try to do it all. Guilt, fear, fatigue, anger, and remorse grease the slope. This night Pete decided to go out; and he took Willie with him.

Dinner is pleasant. The food is good and interesting, and the service is attentive without being intrusive. There aren't many people in the restaurant, and they have a booth under a glass ceiling where they can hear the sound of the rain and watch the water run over their heads and down across the window next to them. It's a soothing environment. The waitress compliments Willie on his white hair. That is probably the high point. Willie does like a compliment.

Over dinner Pete finds himself talking about his relationship with Willie's clinical social worker, Siobhan McFarlane who goes by the nickname Foxy.

"Did I ever tell you how I found out you were living in the High Rise, Willie? It was Foxy. I guess you must have given her my name and, after she helped you move into the High Rise, she sent out emails to every Peter Rangely she could find on the Internet. She likes you Willie, and she wanted to see if she could find any of your family. I'm glad she found me. I guess it's just you and me now Willie."

Pete is used to doing most of the talking when he's with Willie. He thinks it is important to give Willie the opportunity to respond, so their conversations tend to be very one-sided and filled with rhetorical questions. This evening's conversation is particularly one-sided because Pete is feeling his way along in terms of his relationship with Foxy, and, to a large extent, he's thinking out loud.

Foxy is a clinical social worker with a home health care service in Mill River. Her patients are scattered throughout Mill River and the surrounding towns and range from wealthy recluses who live in big houses and have private care around the clock, to bug-eyed schizophrenics who live in the kind of squalor that isn't supposed to exist anywhere in New England. She works with the developmentally impaired, the clinically depressed, patients with multiple personalities, dementia, and Alzheimer's, recovering alcoholics and drug addicts, and an assortment of garden variety psychotics. It's easy to find some justification for Foxy to attend to most of the members of the diverse population of individuals who pass through and around and out of the home healthcare, Medicare/Medicaid system. The medical, social, financial, and personal issues that many of them face are enough to make the most stable person crazy. There is a big demand for clinical social workers, as a result; and there aren't very many of them.

Foxy is in her 50s. She's about 5'6" and in very good shape, although the way she usually dresses in baggy pullovers and khaki pants masks her shapely figure. People tend to notice her red hair, and her blue eyes, and her accent. Foxy speaks with an Irish accent. He realizes as he is talking to Willie that there is a lot he doesn't know about her.

"I've never met anyone like her. Willie. To tell you the truth, I think I came as kind of a surprise to her, too. Life is full of surprises. Don't you think?"

Willie doesn't respond. He seems preoccupied during dinner. If Willie is less talkative than usual, Pete is more.

Willie's movement seems stiff as they leave the restaurant. Pete thinks at first it might be from sitting so long. That isn't it. Willie walks ahead of Pete and when Pete reaches around him to open the door of the van, he snaps, "I don't need you to open my door." He snatches at the handle, but the door is locked. Pete unlocks it and steps back. Willie yanks the door open so hard he almost knocks himself down.

As he steps up into the van, Pete can see The Lip. The Lip is set. Pete wonders if Willie holds his lip like that because he was a saxophone player for decades. Whatever the cause, Willie's stiff upper lip is an unambiguous tell that Willie is upset.

When Pete gets in behind the steering wheel, Willie is already buckled into his seatbelt and staring out the window.

The Dead Woman in His Room

"Let's take a drive, Willie. Want to? It's a nice evening for a drive, don't you think?"

"It's raining."

"Yeah, I like driving in the rain. It's calming, don't you think?" Pete looks over at Willie.

Willie glowers back. "Why are you asking me all these questions? What do you care what I think? You only care about that woman, that red-haired woman. That's all you ever talk about."

Pete is blindsided by Willie's comment. "That's not true, Willie. We talk about a lot of things. I never talked to you about Foxy before. You like Foxy. I thought you'd be interested."

"Well. I'm not." Willie stares into the windshield.

"Well. Okay then. Let's just drive a little."

"You're driving. What choice do I have?"

Pete lets it go. He has learned that arguing with Willie at these times is like arguing with a drunk. It's never productive. He tries not to take these outbursts personally, but it's hard not to. He turns on the windshield wipers and the lights and pulls out of the parking lot. A misty rain makes it look as if they are driving into a tunnel made by their headlights. Within a few miles they are on a rural, two-lane road winding the long way back to Mill River. Pete drives slowly to stay inside the limited visibility. There are very few cars on the road.

Willie is quiet for a long time, and Pete begins to think the ride is working, that his uncle is getting calmer. Driving in the mist makes it feel as if they are floating. He's going slowly and he, at least, is beginning to relax.

"I'm getting out of this car right now," Willie suddenly announces and flings his door open. If it weren't for his seatbelt, he would have made it out the door.

The dome light comes on and the door swings fully open as Pete brakes hard. He grabs at Willie's hand as his uncle reaches for the seatbelt release button.

"Willie! What are you doing? The car's moving. You can't get out here."

"I'm getting out. I don't need you to tell me what to do."

"I'm not telling you anything. This is the middle of nowhere, Willie. You can't get out here."

"Why are you doing this to me?" Willie snarls at Pete. "I never did anything to you. I'm getting out of here. I hate this car. I hate you."

Willie pushes Pete's hand away with his left hand and reaches over with his right to release the seatbelt.

"Willie, stop."

Pete has stopped the van by the side of the road. It's tipped steeply to the right, and Willie's door hangs wide open into the dark. The dome light shines out the door into the rain.

Pete turns to Willie to stop him from getting out of the car, and Willie starts flailing his arms in Pete's face.

"Let me go. Let me go."

Pete leans into Willie and reaches frantically for the seatbelt. With a surprising amount of force, Willie backhands Pete in the mouth with his knuckles. The force of the blow splits his lip and pushes him upright. He puts his hand to his face and feels blood running down his chin. He looks at Willie in amazement.

Willie stops. He looks at Pete. He looks at his hand. He looks out the windshield. He looks out his door into the rain. He sits this way for some time, rubbing his hand.

"Where are we? What are we doing here?" he says. "I want to go home. Why won't you take me home?"

Pete reaches across Willie and closes his door. Then he gets some Kleenex out of the glove compartment and holds it to his lip.

He takes a deep breath. "Let's go home, Willie. Want to?"

"I want to go home."

"Okay, Willie. Okay. Let's do that."

They drive in silence back to the High Rise.

The Dead Woman in His Room

The foyer of the High Rise is empty except for Murph, the security guard who is on the phone when they arrive. Murph waves a cursory acknowledgement as Pete escorts Willie to the elevators.

~~~

That was the worst. The worst so far. Foxy warned him that this kind of thing could happen. Pete believed her, but he thought he could deal with it. He wasn't prepared for feeling so ineffective. It was especially hard because he'd spent the time over dinner caught up in all that was happening between him and Foxy; something else he didn't fully understand. It was as if they were each going through some kind of checklist in their minds and were each amazed to realize that all the checks, so far, were positive.

These were two people who were very happy being alone, or at least resolved to being alone as their choice. They weren't either of them hopeless romantics, but they felt as if they had known each other for a long time. This was a tricky idea for two people who prided themselves on their independence. It was as if they were falling in love, something they had each built elaborate and effective barricades against over the course of many years. It would take a lot to break those down.

5

"I know about HAL Holdings."

It's dark and still raining when Candice parks in front of the River Street Hotel. It looks like the kind of place she associates with winos and whores. If she weren't so worried about protecting Willie, she would never set foot in such a place. She walks up the short flight of stairs and through two sets of double doors into the lobby. A TV is on, and a couple of old men are sitting on a once-green sofa watching the TV…until they see her come in. Then they watch her. The place smells of mold and cigarette smoke.

When the night clerk sees Candice enter he gives her a once-over with his eyes that she can almost feel. She is an extremely capable person who is comfortable almost any place in the world, but she has no direct experience with places like this.

"I wonder if you would tell me if a Peter Rangely is one of your guests," Candice asks, her anxiety contributing to an excess of formality.

"Pete? Maybe. Who wants to know?"

"I am a friend…of the family," Candice says. "Do you have any idea when he might return?"

"Well, we might have a Peter Rangely here, and he might return. You could wait for him in our spacious lobby…" The clerk waves his hand in a sweeping motion to indicate the sitting area with the two old men. "Or back here with me." He smiles, pulling back a curtain to reveal the cot in the back office.

"I don't think so," Candice says. She approaches the front desk and puts her hand in her purse. "I wonder if I could wait for Mr. Rangely in his room. It's very important that I see him as soon as he comes back." She puts her hand on the counter, partially covering a $50 bill.

"It would be my pleasure," the clerk says, putting his hand on top of hers and then drawing his fingers slowly along the length of her fingers, pulling the bill out from under her hand, and, in the process, sending shivers of revulsion up her arm. She looks up and sees he has a name tag. His name is Vinny.

Candice steps back. Vinny looks at her while he folds the bill in half, tucks it into the right front pocket of his tight chino pants, and then pats his pocket affectionately.

"May I have the key to his room, please," she says.

"Oh, allow me," he says, grabbing a key from the hooks behind his stool and coming out from behind the counter. He is actually shorter than she is. She realizes he must have been standing on a raised platform to make himself look taller. "Creep." She feels a little less afraid of him.

"After you," he says, indicating the stairs that lead up to a landing on his right.

She can feel his eyes on her as she climbs the stairs. At one point she has the horrifying thought that there might not be a Peter Rangely in the River Street Hotel, and that she is allowing herself to be led to some filthy backroom where this nasty little man will try to rape her.

"Ahem." She hears Vinny's voice behind her. He stopped at the top of the stairs and watched her walk part way down the corridor away from him. "Mr. Rangely's room is 209," he says. He opens the door and stands watching her as she walks toward him. "One of our better rooms. It has a bed with a new mattress."

The Dead Woman in His Room

She looks down at him and jerks the key from his hand. "I won't be staying."

She shuts the door in his face, realizing only then that there are no lights on in the room. She feels panic rise until her hand finds the switch by the door.

The room is messy, but not dirty. It looks like a graduate student might live here. There is a small bathroom off to the right and on the other side of the bathroom wall there is a kitchenette. Straight ahead is an art deco breakfast table with two chairs. They are from a set, but they're mismatched. Each has a gray stripe across the back of the seat, but one is yellow and one orange. The seats of both chairs are cracked, and stuffing bulges out in several places.

Most of the top of the table is covered by a computer monitor and keyboard. As she walks into the room, she sees a book on Alzheimer's disease and a mystery novel open on the table. There is also a plastic cereal bowl with a spoon in it.

Deeper into the room, the bed extends out from the wall on the right. It isn't made but the covers are pulled over the pillows, probably by Pete. Candice guesses they don't offer much in the way of housekeeping at the River Street Hotel.

She can see the streetlights seeping through Venetian blinds on the window straight ahead. There's a frumpy looking easy chair just to the left of the window in the corner with two crates set on top of each other next to it to form a makeshift bookcase. On the left wall—where it would be in-line with the bed—is a TV on a wire cart. She notices the TV is not plugged in.

Candice forces herself to walk the full length of the room. She bends the blinds down with her finger to look out the window which looks over River Street. It has stopped raining.

As she turns back toward the room, she realizes that she has rubbed dust off on her finger and reaches in her purse for a Kleenex. She feels safer for having completed her tour of the room. This is obviously not the room of a wino or a whore, although it may have once been. She is able to get a sense of the person who lives here, and her sense is that Pete is a thoughtful person, certainly a reader, judging from the number of open books around the room. The crates, although they are crates, are lined up neatly. Beyond them is a big plastic file drawer, the kind that has a lid, so you can stack others on top of it.

She walks back toward the kitchen area. Somewhat more relaxed now, she becomes aware of details she missed on her way through to the window. A photo of Willie catches her eye. It is held to the front of the refrigerator by magnets. She bends down to look at it. Willie is standing in front of what she assumes is Pete's van. She recognizes the parking lot at the High Rise. Willie looks frail to her. She touches the picture gently with her fingertips. Next to the photo is a primitive drawing of a red-headed woman done with colored pencils. She can tell the sketch was not drawn by a child. Along the top of the stove there are boxes of different kinds of tea. There isn't a teapot, but there is an empty saucepan with a tea ball in it.

Candice is less afraid. This isn't the room of a scary person. She thinks maybe she could see Willie's nephew staying in a place like this. She had actually read a couple of his books. They were interesting, if a little esoteric.

She sits down in the orange chair with the gray streak where she can watch the door for Pete's arrival.

~~~

Candice has never been in a place like this, but Nick, Jr. has. Many times. He's been with whores in places like this. Places like this are like his home. He hates places like this, but he knows them inside and out. The smells, the sounds, the stained brown carpet, the back entrances, the locks. Places like these are nothing but open doors to Nick, Jr.

Nick, Jr. followed Candice to the River Street Hotel from the High Rise and parked down the street where he could watch the front of the building. He has no idea why she has come to Mill

River, but he knows that she is connected to Kyle, and he can tell by the way she moves that she is afraid. He can see fear from a distance, almost like an aura. This is the place she bolted to from New Orleans—with nothing but a briefcase. She has to be meeting someone. Someone who also knows about HAL. Her fear tells him that she has heard about Kyle.

Nick, Jr. is a very good killer, but he isn't good at figuring things out. When he's given a job, he doesn't have to know why his targets did whatever they did. That has all been figured out by someone else. He doesn't have to get information from them. He just has to study their behavior long enough to spot an opportunity. And take it.

This is an opportunity. If it had been a private house or a better-quality hotel, he would have waited ... but a flea-bag hotel. This is too easy. She's in his world. This is like when he used to kill rabbits in their hutches just to smell the fear and feel them die in his hands. It wasn't that different, really. Killing a person. Actually, he didn't hate rabbits. That made killing them a little harder. He did that to harden himself when he was 13; after he and his sister and mother were tossed into the barrio like trash, and he had to teach himself to be hard. He's very hard now.

He only waits a few minutes in front of the boarding house when he sees the light go on in a room on the second floor. No one else has entered the building, so he's pretty sure this Constance woman is there. A few minutes later, he sees her look out through the blinds.

Nick slides out of his car. Before heading behind the hotel, he goes to Candice's rental car and uses a Slim Jim to pop open the passenger side door. He wants to be sure to get her briefcase, which she hadn't taken with her. He can tell it has a laptop computer in it. He slides the briefcase under a dumpster behind the hotel where he can grab it in a hurry later. Then he lets himself in through the back door. It isn't even locked. Typical.

When Candice hears someone at the door fumbling with the lock, she assumes it's Pete. She's been in the room long enough to calm down, somewhat, and is running over in her mind what she will say to him. She never met Pete and has no idea what he looks like, but she expects to see some family resemblance to Willie. Maybe Willie will be with him.

Nick enters the room so quickly and smoothly that she hardly sees him before he is standing next to her with his hand on the back of her neck and a knife in her face. She sees he has on surgical gloves.

"I know about HAL Holdings. I need the access codes. Now."

"What? Who are you!?"

"Wrong answer," Nick slides the knife blade gently down the side of her right cheek. It doesn't hurt, but she can feel it start to bleed. He shows her the knife. There is blood on it. Hers.

"HAL Holdings. Access codes. While you still have a face."

"I don't have the codes with me."

"But you have them."

In her panic, Candice is still able to hear the question in his statement. He didn't know much about HAL. How did he know anything about HAL?

"I have the codes, and I can give them to you. I am the only person who can give them to you." She turns in his hand to look up at him.

Nick isn't good at this. He hasn't thought it all through. He needs access codes. She has them. She should give them to him. He would kill her. There wouldn't be all this talking.

Fucking rabbits. They're all fucking rabbits. He could smell the fear.

"Where are they?"

"I don't have them with me. Not here," her fear adds to a tone of incredulity.

"You think I'm stupid."

The Dead Woman in His Room

"I don't think you're stupid. I don't know anything about you." Candice talks in hopes of distracting him. "There are different codes for different people. Who are you? I need to know who you are to give you the right codes." She's making this up.

"I'm Nick Baron's kid. His money belongs to me. I need his codes. Where are they?"

"Nick Barons!" she is genuinely surprised. "I didn't know he had any kids. He never said he had kids."

"I'm the beaner kid he wished he never had. I was his nightmare, and now I'm your nightmare. I'm going to ask you one more time. Where are the codes?"

"They're in my briefcase. In my laptop." This is actually true. "My computer."

"I know what a fucking laptop is."

Nick vacillates. It is believable that the codes are in the laptop. Everything is in a laptop. He also knows where the laptop is. And she doesn't.

He tightens his grip on the back of her neck and lifts her to her feet. "You're coming with me."

"You can't hurt me. You need me to get your codes. You need me alive."

Above all she did not want to leave this room with this man.

He sets the knife blade back on her cheek.

"How much you want to bet?" he says.

She jerks away, and as she does, the knife slides down the side of her face. Not just a little cut this time. A big one. Her cheek opens up and blood starts pouring out, running down her neck.

"Fuck." He grabs her by her shoulder and shoves her on his knife which enters her chest just below her solar plexus. He could feel her breasts. She dies quickly in his hands, and he lets her slide to the floor.

He is more excited by this killing. He stands over her. The knife in his hand. Then he sees that he has her blood on him. Not much, but some. He tries to never do that. Never get blood on himself. Even though he always kills with a knife. Mostly his victims don't bleed much. The deep gash in her face was an accident. Her fault.

He's losing track of time. This seems to be taking too long. He looks around quickly for anything that would tell him about the person who lives in this room. On the refrigerator door he sees a photo of an old man standing in front of a van. That could be the guy she went to see at the High Rise. He recognizes the parking lot. He pulls the photo off the door and puts it in his pocket. Then he pulls out the drawers from the bureau and stacks them on the bed, going quickly through each one, looking for something that would have this guy's name on it. He throws the clothes on the floor. On top of Candice. Nothing. He finds nothing. He looks at the PC monitor on the table in disgust and sweeps the books on the floor. He takes her purse and jams it into his jacket pocket.

Then he hears the front door of the boarding house open beneath him.

"Hey, Pete." He hears the night clerk say. "There's a woman in your room. No, really. Nice ass, too. You sneaky dog."

He doesn't hear the rest. He turns off the light and is out of the room and down the hall, retracing his steps out the back of the boarding house. In the darkness behind the boarding house, he slides the briefcase from under the dumpster where he left it. He doesn't need her. He has her laptop. Who's stupid now?

~~~

Nick drives for more than an hour. He wants to get far away from Mill River, and he needs to calm down. He wouldn't have stopped at all that night, but he wants to boot up the laptop and find the access codes. He's sure they'll be there, but he wants to see them with his own eyes. She couldn't know that he already had her laptop. He feels superior. Stupid white cunt. He stops at a rest stop and beats off mechanically into the grass. He feels better. He's calmer now.

The Dead Woman in His Room

Somewhere in upstate New York he checks into a motel with several tractor trailers parked around it. He pays cash in advance for his room. He's already shifted everything, including his shirt with the blood on it into a duffle bag. When he checks in, he has on a T-shirt and blue jeans, like 99 percent of the guests.

The first thing Nick does when he gets in the room is turn on the TV and then wash the blood out of his clothes with a mixture of liquid hand soap and ammonia that he carries with him. He is very disciplined. He tossed the knife at the rest stop. He always uses cheap knives, and he always cleans them and throws them away afterwards. You didn't need anything fancy to kill a person. Some guys got attached to their knives. That was stupid.

Nick takes the laptop out of the briefcase and sets it on the bed. The power cord is wrapped up neatly next to it in the case and he unwinds it and plugs it into the wall socket. He trained himself to be very methodical around computers. It didn't come naturally to him.

Hers is an IBM ThinkPad. He's seen a lot of those. He boots it up and is asked for a password. Fuck. There was always a way around a password, but this could take a while. He takes a deep breath and looks at the screen. There's a blinking red text box with a message: "You have 10 seconds to enter the correct password, or all data will be destroyed." He's never seen that before.

He watches in horror as a digital counter appears on the screen. It's counting down from 5. He doesn't know what to do. He watches transfixed as the counter reaches 0, and the screen goes dark. He can hear the hard drive racing…erasing, he realizes. He hits "delete," he hits "escape," he hits three keys together: "control," "alt," "delete." Nothing works. He pulls the plug. It keeps racing. He wants to reach inside and grab the hard drive and make it stop. Battery, battery. He flips it over and looks frantically for the battery slot. The PC card pops out. He claws at the corners. "Where the fuck is the battery!"

The Dead Woman in His Room

It stops.

He pushes the button to boot it up. Nothing happens. He plugs the power cord back in. Nothing.

One time in prison after he'd been in a fight, the guards locked him in a crawl space in a section of the cell block that was used for storage. It was too short to sit up and not long enough to lie down. He had to lay in a fetal position on his left side. He couldn't even turn over. It was completely dark. They left him there for two days.

This was like that. He realizes he's been yelling, not words, just yelling.

The banging on the wall brings him back. "Shut up. Asshole. Shut the fuck up." He hears through the wall. The rest of the night he sits on the floor at the foot of his bed in the motel rocking back and forth. The TV blaring in the background.

In the morning, Nick stuffs everything back into his duffle bag and drives back to Mill River. That bitch went to see two people: one at the apartment building and the guy in the boarding house. He still has them.

6

"She was here when I got here."

Vinny, the night clerk, seems to be waiting for him when Pete walks through the dirty double doors into the lobby of the River Street Hotel.

"Hey, Pete," Vinny calls over to him. "There's a woman in your room. Really. Nice ass, too. You sneaky dog."

Pete is pretty non-judgmental and can usually find something to like in just about anyone, but he really doesn't care for Vinny. The guy's a creep and his constant sexual allusions are tedious at best. Pete usually feels a need to wash his hands after talking with Vinny.

"Yeah, right. Sure, Vinny," Pete says, passing quickly through the lobby toward the stairs. He keeps his hand over his mouth, so Vinny won't see his split lip. He doesn't want to have to explain anything to Vinny.

When he starts up the stairs, he hears someone in the hall above him and pauses long enough to hear the footsteps lead away toward the back of the hotel. He doesn't want to talk to anyone this night. He's worried about leaving Willie alone and plans to go back to the High Rise and sleep on Willie's couch. While he's stopped on the stairs he takes the key to his room out of his pocket. It's one of the old-fashioned keys attached to a big red plastic tear-drop fob with the room number 209 etched into it.

The Dead Woman in His Room

Pete opens his door distractedly and is confronted by a scene of unfamiliar turmoil. His first reaction is to say, "Excuse me," and step back into the hall, as if he entered someone else's room by mistake. He closes the door. Looks at the key fob in his hand. Looks at the number on the door. Looks down the hall. It's quiet. He opens the door again. This time he pushes it open far enough to look inside. He can only see part of one wall of the room, and the table with his computer on it. Then he sees the book he was reading on the floor by the table. It's lying fanned out on its pages with the spine up. It occurs to him he will have lost his place. The thought irritates him, and he steps into the room, lets the door close behind him and bends down to pick up the book. As he stands up, he becomes aware of something on the other side of the table. It's the dead woman.

She's a mess. Blood is all over her clothes and, he realizes, all over his clothes which were thrown across her and around the room. The bureau drawers were pulled out and stacked. Pete remembers being struck by the fact that the empty drawers were stacked, as if with some care. How could someone do this to a person and then take the time to stack the drawers?

As messed up as the dead woman is, Pete knows he doesn't know her. She's not young, but she obviously kept herself well. Through the horror of her, he can tell her clothes are very stylish and expensive. She was beautiful; whoever she was. Although this is his room, and his clothes and his papers are scattered in her blood, he has the profound feeling that the dead woman has nothing to do with him.

Pete stands up. He doesn't feel a thing, at first. He just looks. Frozen. He can almost see himself standing there looking. Feeling nothing. He doesn't know what to do. Part of him wants to start cleaning up the room. He resists that part. Part of him wants to stare at the body. From where he is standing, he has to lean forward and look over the table to see her body sprawled on the floor. She is fully dressed, but her skirt is hiked up. He looks away, a spasm of politeness as if he opened a bathroom door on a stranger. He takes a breath and steps off to the side where he doesn't have to lean over the table to see her. She looks as if she'd just been dropped there, discarded. His clothes must have been thrown on the floor after she was killed. A t-shirt of his partially covers her left arm. She's wearing a gold necklace and earrings.

Then he sees her eyes. Her eyes are open. He exhales involuntarily and looks away. His stuff is everywhere, but it all seems unfamiliar. He looks at the window. The blinds are closed and the light from the street filters through the curtains. There may have been a breeze, but the windows are sealed shut. He hates the fact that hotel windows are always sealed shut, even in old hotels like this one. The thought seems so inappropriate he almost laughs. The circumstances make all his thoughts seem inappropriate. He feels awkward and just stands there. Then he starts to cry involuntarily. He put his hands over his mouth and nose, and weeps. He just stands there alone and cries and takes deep gulping breaths. And he has no idea why. He must have stood there, just inside the door, for a long time. Then he calls 911.

"This is Peter Rangely in room 209 of the River Street Hotel. There is a dead woman in my room…No. I am the only one here, besides her. Yes. I will stay here. No. I do not know who she is. She was here when I got here. Please hurry. Yes. I will stay here."

Pete takes another deep breath. Then he hears sirens. Then the police arrive. He hears them clambering up the stairs. The first to arrive is Lieutenant Dominick Petruzio, a big guy with a big belly. He fills the doorway. He enters the room slowly and does something that hadn't occurred to Pete: he turns on the overhead light. Pete feels as if he's suddenly had the wind knocked out of him. He gulps for air and turns back to look at the officer in the doorway.

Faces appear around his shape, looking in. They look like balloons. One of them is Vinny. Another is Detective Rick

Henderson. Petruzio walks over to the body, grunts, and walks immediately back toward the door, seeming to push people back outside by his approach.

"Get these people out of here," he says to Henderson.

"This your room?" he says to Pete without looking at him. He's moving around the room looking at everything else. He flips open a small notebook.

"Yeah."

"Who is she?"

"I don't know."

"Uh huh. You found her here?"

"Yes."

Each time Pete answers a question, Petruzio looks down at his note pad, but Pete notices, he doesn't write anything. "You didn't touch anything?" he asks.

"No."

"This your stuff?"

"Yes."

"Tell me…you're Rangely, right? Pete Rangely. You're the one who called?

"Yeah."

"Tell me Mr. Rangely, Vinny, the night clerk said that ten or 15 minutes must have transpired after he saw you in the lobby and before you called 911. What happened during that time, Mr. Rangely?"

The question strikes Pete as odd. It also doesn't seem possible that that much time had elapsed. "I don't know. I got here. I found her, and then I called 911."

"Okay." Petruzio leans closer. "You all right? Your eyes are red. Were you crying? Why were you crying, Mr. Rangely? Do you know this woman?"

"No. I don't know who she is. I don't think I was crying. I don't know. It was a shock. Maybe."

"Maybe what?"

The Dead Woman in His Room

"Maybe I was crying. I don't know. Why do you ask?"

"Oh, I don't know. There's a dead woman in your room. The night clerk says you were here for a good 15 minutes before you called 911. At least some of that time, you were standing here crying; and you have a fat lip. It looks like somebody popped you good. How did you get that fat lip, Mr. Rangely? Could it have been her? Maybe? You had a fight, she hit you, you lashed out…something like that? Is that what happened."

"No. No. I didn't do this." Pete is taken completely off guard by the implications of what Petruzio is saying. "She was dead when I got here. She didn't hit me. My uncle hit me. My uncle Willie. He's got Alzheimer's and he was trying to unbuckle his seatbelt. He wanted to get out of the van, but it was still moving. I was trying to stop him when he hit me in the mouth."

"Your uncle?"

"Yes."

"While he was trying to get out of your van?"

"Yes.

"While your van was still moving?"

"Yes. It was moving. We were coming home from dinner. We had dinner together at the Portuguese restaurant in Edgemont. You can ask them. We were there. I'm sure they'll remember us."

"Oh, we'll ask them. Don't worry about that. When was that, by the way? When did you leave the restaurant?"

"I don't know exactly. Around 8 o'clock."

"Okay. Maybe 8 o'clock. Then what happened?"

"We drove around for quite a while. I often take my uncle for rides. It seems to calm him…usually it calms him."

"Except this night he punched you in the mouth?"

"He didn't punch me exactly. It was an accident. He was trying to get out of his seatbelt, and I was trying to stop him."

"This is while the car is still moving."

"Yes."

"While you were driving around for hours after dinner?"

"Yes."

"Where is your uncle now?"

"He's in the High Rise. Room 509. But he's got Alzheimer's. He's not going to remember anything."

"Well. What do you know? Not much of an alibi, is it Mr. Rangely?"

"Oh, come on. I didn't kill this woman. I don't even know who she is."

"Uh huh. You've got to admit, it looks a little suspicious."

"Oh, for Christ's sake."

"What! What did you just say?"

Pete takes a deep breath. "Look. I'm sorry. I'm tired. It's been a long day."

"Yeah. I suppose it has been a long day," Petruzio says looking over at the body. He turns back to look at Pete. "And it ain't over yet, Mr. Rangely. Not by a long shot."

"Rick. Rick," Petruzio calls out. When officer Henderson opens the door, Petruzio says, "Take Mr. Rangely down to the station. We're going to need to talk some more after I check this out. Oh, and Rick. Better read Mr. Rangely his rights."

"Yes, sir," Henderson says. He likes reading people their rights.

~~~

Except for the hum of florescent lights, it's quiet in the interrogation room at the station. Pete sits at a wooden table and looks away from the wall with the one-way mirror. He's exhausted. He's also very aware that he can't leave, and he's anxious about Willie by himself at the High Rise. He puts his hands over his face and sucks in a deep breath. Then he runs his fingers through the hair on the side of his head, and massages the top of his head, a nervous habit. He folds and unfolds his arms and looks at the initials scratched into the tabletop. Why the hell would anyone carve their initials in this table?

Pete isn't thinking about the dead woman in his room. He's thinking about the last time he was inside a police interrogation room. It was a long time ago in San Francisco. He was drunk and had been in a fight. His daughter had been with him. She was just three and a half. The police had taken her away, and word had spread that he was a child abuser. He'd been beaten, first by the other prisoners in the holding tank; and then by the police in the interrogation room. He couldn't remember what had happened; why he'd been arrested. He had to ask himself if he could have done what they said. He asked himself, over and over again. He didn't think so.

No charges were filed that time and Pete was released early the next morning. His relationship had not been good with his wife, Ellen, for some time leading up to this incident. A month later Ellen took their daughter and went back home to Phoenix, Arizona. Pete let them go. That was a very dark time. He signed the divorce papers when they arrived some months later. His wife said she thought it best if he stay away. Staying away was pretty much what he had done ever since. That was 20 years ago.

~~~

"That guy's weird," Henderson says when Petruzio joins him in the coffee room in the police station. "You think he did it?"

"Maybe."

"I think he did it. I bet they were lovers, and he killed her. You said he'd been crying. Why would he be crying over someone he didn't even know? I don't buy that. Do you?"

Henderson wasn't Petruzio's favorite partner of all time. He was like a little fox terrier: over-eager and head strong. Smart but not observant. Everything was a big deal to Henderson. He wanted to be a cop all his life, but most of his career, such as it was, he was a security guard. After the Mill River police department hired him, they realized he was too scrawny to be very convincing on patrol, so they decided to try him on investigations, and they made Petruzio take him on as a partner. Petruzio hated the fact that now he had to figure out what to do with Henderson just because the police commissioner put pressure on the chief to hire more cops. "Wouldn't occur to them to hire the right person in the first place," Petruzio muttered to his wife Maureen on more than a few occasions. "Assholes." He didn't say that last part out loud…around his wife.

Petruzio subscribes to the popular cop dictum that there are only three kinds of people: cops, cops' families, and assholes. It simplifies things. Some judgment calls have to be made around the fringes—Petruzio, for example, isn't yet sure if Henderson is a cop or an asshole, and he has some serious misgivings about the police commissioner, but, for the most part, Petruzio can live with that level of uncertainty. It's a progressive attitude in a way: it doesn't matter if you are white or black, Mexican, or Asian, rich, or poor. If you aren't a cop or a member of a cop's family, you're an asshole. All the kinds of terrible things that Petruzio had seen people do to each other in 28 years of police work were made a little easier to take. They were just assholes. Except for young kids. Petruzio hated when something bad happened to young kids. Anybody else could have deserved what they got. You never knew the whole story.

Petruzio is an effective detective because he knows he'll never know all the details of a case. Recognizing that his understanding of a case will always be limited keeps him from jumping to conclusions. He has to be talked into conclusions—unlike Henderson. Henderson is probably an asshole. He certainly isn't much of a cop at this point.

~~~

The cops are able to find out a surprisingly small amount of information about the dead woman in Pete's hotel room. The name on the rental car agreement was Constance DeBreaux who, as far as they could tell had sprung to life in New Orleans in the late 1970s as an independently wealthy private investor. It was as if her personal record had been deleted before 1978.

The Dead Woman in His Room

"Maybe she's CIA. Do you think she could be like an operative or something?" Henderson wanted to know. "I bet she's some kind a spook."

"Jesus, Rick. You watch too many movies." Petruzio says, rubbing his eyes under his reading glasses. He's sitting at the computer screen in the stationhouse. He knows how to use the computer, but he doesn't like computer research. He prefers working with clues that he can see and touch and even smell. He would sometimes pick up evidence from a crime scene and sniff it like a hound dog. He looks a little like a hound dog, actually.

"You ever learn anything from sniffing evidence like that," Henderson asked him one time when Petruzio hadn't realized he was being watched.

"Yeah," he said. "I learned police work stinks."

A few days later, Petruzio is amused to see Henderson take a wallet that had been found at a crime scene and sniff it all around like a little terrier.

Petruzio hasn't been able to find any connection between this Constance woman and Pete other than that she was found dead in Pete's hotel room. They didn't find the murder weapon.

Pete's police record is a pretty short story. He was first fingerprinted when he was arrested in 1971 at a peace rally in San Francisco. He was arrested a couple of years later for drunk and disorderly conduct, but the charges were dropped. Petruzio made a mental note to have Henderson look into the story behind that event. Other than that, and a few speeding tickets, Pete Rangely appears to be pretty much what he says he is: a freelance writer. Petruzio can't say "freelance writer" without disdain sounding in his voice. Petruzio is not a big reader. He finds references to several books that Pete wrote, but the local library has none of them.

To his surprise, a background check on Rangely's uncle Willie Lyons reveals that he also appears to have no past on record beyond 1978. "Maybe they're both in the CIA?" he jokes to himself. The coincidence troubles him, however.

7

"So, what do you want from me?"

Nick never stays in a town where he's done a job. There is never any need to. He's a specialist. His job is the killing, and when it's done he leaves. This time, however, his job wasn't the killing—that had just happened—and he wasn't done. In fact, he has to admit, the killing made his job harder.

Nick always works alone, but this is the first time he's working for himself. He knows he needs to be smart, and he has a kind of animal smartness that makes him a good killer. But he's a lousy planner. He can watch. He can wait. He can strike with extreme ruthlessness. But he can't develop a strategy beyond killing. He isn't really sure what to do.

Nick books a room in a motel off the Interstate about 20 miles north of Mill River. He tells them at check-in that he's a salesman and might be in town as long as a week. He pays for three nights in cash. He cleans and returns the rental car he was driving and rents a small U-Rent van. U-Rent vans are good for stakeouts. Not only can you sit in the back in darkness, so no one can see you, but the U-Rent name is so ubiquitous it makes the van itself essentially invisible.

Unsure what else to do, Nick resorts to his two primary skills: he can watch, and he can wait. The boarding house is crawling with cops, so he sets up a few vantage points where he can watch the comings and goings at the High Rise.

The Dead Woman in His Room

These kinds of buildings are a problem for Nick. They have limited access. They have security guards and security cameras. There are never enough elevators, and they're always slow. No one ever takes the stairs, so if he does, he feels extremely exposed. It's hard to be quiet in metal stairwells. They also reminded him of prison. Nick learned to be ruthless in prison, but those lessons came from the ruthlessness that was done to him. He survived, but he has many scars. Anything that reminds him of prison triggers a survival instinct that is frighteningly effective, if not rational. He does not want to have to go into this building.

So, he watches, and he waits. He needs information. He doesn't know who the woman he killed went to see in the High Rise. He assumes it was the guy in the picture he took from the hotel room. He needs someone who can come and go in the High Rise and get him information. He hates being in this position. He hates having to depend on someone else. It always means killing someone else. It's always messy.

Nick watches the High Rise. Moving his location, so he won't become obvious. He tries to put himself in the state of mind he experienced as a child when he could watch and wait almost indefinitely. He just observes. It's a kind of meditation. He isn't angry in that place, but he's having trouble finding it.

Mostly he watches old people come and go and gets a sense of the rhythm of the High Rise. That's how he first happens to notice Kenny. Kenny is out of rhythm. Residents of the High Rise tend to wake up early. Most of them are old and have lost, or never had, the ability to sleep late. Lights start coming on any time after 5 am. Over the course of the next few hours, residents start coming out of the building in ones and twos—some to stretch and walk the paved trail that meanders 1/4 mile through the grounds. Some head directly for a favorite bench where they set up camp for the morning. Some just stand in the doorway as if the arrival of another day is an event worth noting in person. By late morning, there is very little activity; those who are coming out are out and in their respective positions.

Similarly, between about 4 and 6 pm there's another period of relative activity as people make their way back to their apartments to prepare for dinner. There is very little activity after dinner. Most people are in for the night. The darkness is not the friend of the elderly.

Nick first sees Kenny at night; around 9:30 pm. Kenny is setting out in his slightly spastic gate, heading toward the north side of town. He has on a roadie jacket with the name of some punk band on the back. His hair is thin on top, but he wears it tied in back in a greasy ponytail. Kenny walks with his shoulders hunched together against the chill September night. Nick can spot an ex-junkie. He can also spot a snitch. This guy is a snitch. This guy is an ex-junkie snitch. Bingo. Maybe he's finally going to get a break.

~~~

Nick follows Kenny that night and gets a tour of the fringe of the Mill River drug culture. Like a lot of mill towns, everything flows to the river in Mill River. From the High Rise on the west side of town, Kenny takes a circuitous route through the parking lot at the new Super Shop which occupies a kind of plateau cut out from where an old factory had burned down. Super Shop shares the parking lot with a Chinese restaurant, a video store, and a few other shops.

Teenagers fill the shadows around the edges, trolling for something to do, some on skateboards, some in cars, some just standing in small groups, not talking. They don't come for the stores. They came for the parking lot.

Kenny is making his rounds like a homeless dog, staying in the shadows, and sniffing out easy opportunities. He knows a lot of these kids. Nick hears one of them call him "Kenny."

Nick knows this kind. He could be very useful. He would know who everyone is and what they do and where they are weak. And not just in the fringe drug world. He'd also know the cops. They would have used him. Drugs and money for information. The police allow guys like this one to exist, so they can serve as their eyes and ears on the street. He uses them that way, too.

He could also be dangerous, Nick knows. Kenny would be a coward which would mean he'd be ready to bolt at the least sign of danger and would switch his allegiance according to which of his two primary emotions was stronger: fear or greed. Nick would attract him with greed and hold him with fear. He knew how to do that. Something else he'd learned in the penitentiary.

Nick is good at working people like Kenny because he isn't a coward, and he isn't motivated by greed. He gets paid well for what he does, but he would do it for less. He likes it. He has no loyalty except to his anger, and, at this point, that loyalty is unquestioned. It's who he is.

Nick likes to take more time setting up a guy like this, but he is uncharacteristically impatient. The next night, after following Kenny's tour, Nick can't wait any longer. This guy will have to do.

Nick positions himself on a dark spot along what he has come to see is Kenny's regular route. He'll let Kenny come to him.

When Kenny sees a big guy standing on the sidewalk on the section of Oak Street that passes under a railroad trestle, he almost doesn't go down that way. A detour would mean walking several blocks to get to where there's a bridge over the tracks, and, at this point, Kenny is more lazy than afraid. Mill River was cut in two by the tracks back when trains carried materials to the factories and took finished goods away. The trains don't run now, but the tracks still divide the town.

Kenny walks quickly, staying on the street side of the sidewalk.

"You Kenny?" Nick says when Kenny gets even with him on the sidewalk.

Kenny moves beyond Nick before responding. "Maybe."

"I've got a proposition for a guy named Kenny."

The Dead Woman in His Room

Kenny takes another step away. "Hey, if you're looking for a blow job, I ain't your guy."

Nick lets him move further away. "I'm looking for a source of information," he says. "I thought you might be able to help."

Kenny hesitates. He almost runs when Nick turns to face him, and he sees something in his hand. Then he sees it's a $100 bill, folded in half. He hasn't seen one of those in a long time.

"What kind of information?" Kenny says.

"I need some information on one of your neighbors in the building where you live."

"The High Rise?"

"Yeah. The High Rise."

"Here's some information for free," Kenny said. "There's nobody in the High Rise worth a hundred bucks." He starts to turn away.

"There's a lot of money in Medicare, if you know where to look." Nick says matter-of-factly. "Money and drugs."

"Okay." Kenny says, turning back, but not getting any closer. "So, what are you? A Medicare cop?"

"Not exactly. I work for an organization that used to employ one of your neighbors in the High Rise. We are an alternate distribution source for prescription drugs."

"Legal drugs sold illegally?"

"Something like that. Our business is kind of an after-market in pharmaceuticals: Percocet, Vicodin, OxyContin." Nick pulls a small bottle from his pocket and tosses it to Kenny.

The pills rattle in the bottle when Kenny catches it. He turns it over and looks at the label. It says OxyContin. Kenny loves OxyContin.

"So, what do you want from me?"

"This neighbor of yours has gone off on his own, and my people don't like that sort of thing. We like to keep everything under one roof, our roof. It's more manageable that way; better business. We're businesspeople."

The Dead Woman in His Room

Kenny is still looking at the little bottle in his hand. Moving very smoothly, Nick grabs Kenny's hand in his, and, with just enough force to show his physical strength, he pulls Kenny's hand in front of him palm up. Then he sets the $100 bill next to the pill bottle in Kenny's hand and slowly folds his fingers closed over it.

"So, who's this neighbor?" Kenny asks.

Nick pulls the photo of Willie that he took from Pete's apartment out of his shirt pocket and holds it out to Kenny without saying anything.

"Willie!?" Kenny laughs. "You gotta be fucking kidding me. This guy couldn't find his ass with both hands."

"Looks can be deceiving."

"They'd have to be real deceiving. This guy had a one-way ticket to the nursing home until his nephew showed up a couple of months ago."

"Yeah. What's his name? The nephew?"

"Pete. Pete something. I don't know. Hey, grab a copy of yesterday's paper. He's on the front page. Cops found a dead broad in his room, and he's the prime suspect." Kenny looks abruptly down at his hand. "That must have happened before you got here," he adds.

"Yeah. Must have," Nick says.

Kenny doesn't look up.

"Think about it," Nick says. "All I need to know is whatever you can tell me about this guy." He points to the photo he holds in front of Kenny. "And anybody he's associated with, including his nephew Pete." Nick points to Kenny's hand. "Consider that a down payment."

Nick looks directly at Kenny. "This goes no further than you and me. You understand that?"

"Of course," Kenny says. "Of course. You're the boss."

"Don't forget, my friend" Nick says, then he turns abruptly and walks away.

The Dead Woman in His Room

~ ~ ~

Kenny watches him walk away and then hurries off in the opposite direction. He guesses this scary guy had something to do with the dead woman who is still the talk of the town in Mill River. Kenny doesn't want to get involved in anything as heavy as that, and he tells himself that part of the reason he went along was just to get away without provoking the guy. The other part was the $100 bill, something he hadn't held in his hand in a long time; and the OxyContin. Kenny loves OxyContin. No pain, no fear, no nothing. His girlfriend Jen has a prescription for Oxy for back pain, but, after he made her refill her prescription before it was due, Jen's doctor stopped giving her more than a few doses at a time. Fucking doctors.

As he walks back to the High Rise that night, Kenny's mind races. He still holds the money and the drugs in his right hand which he shoved into the pocket of his jacket. Keeping his right hand in his pocket unsettles his already shaky balance, but he will not release his grip on his prize and, swaying occasionally, he skitters through the dark streets back to the High Rise.

He considers his options: he could take the money and go away for a few days. He doesn't like that option. He's gotten pretty used to Jen's apartment in the High Rise, and he doesn't feel like going anywhere. Inertia always plays a part in Kenny's strategizing.

He could go to the police and tell them about this guy, but he doesn't even know the guy's name at this point. He'd have to know more about him before he could get anything from the cops.

He knows he can't give back the money or the drugs. That would be provoking the guy. Besides, he's planning on taking the drugs as soon as he gets back to the apartment.

Nothing to do but play along, he concludes. Jen knows something about this guy Pete and the old guy Willie. He finds it hard to believe that Willie could be involved in any kind of scam.

The Dead Woman in His Room

He doesn't think Willie can find his way to the end of the hall and back.

Kenny decides to pick Jen's brains a little and see what she knows. He can't imagine what an old loser like Willie could possibly have done to get a scary guy like this one on his trail. He sure as hell wouldn't want that guy after him.

8

"And take those beaner kids with you!"

The first guy Nick killed was Freddie Haskell, a friend of his father's. It was at South Winds, a development of five- and ten-acre ranchettes that Nick's father owned along the foothills 20 miles south of Denver. The Haskells owned the second house built at South Winds. The first house was built by Nick's father. It was the model house for the development: a cedar mansion, cantilevered off a rocky outcrop. It had five bedrooms and featured a three-story wall of windows on the west side that opened on to a multi-level deck facing the mountains. Nick, Jr. had grown up there, until the divorce. He was the first kid in the neighborhood; he and his sister Elizabeth who was four years younger. He loved it there. He was homeschooled by his mother, but he had an Australian Shepard dog and a pinto pony and a backyard that seemed to go on forever.

Nick, Jr. was 12 when his mother picked up him and his sister at a local park in March and, instead of driving home to South Winds, drove them toward Denver. She didn't offer an explanation for a long time. She was driving very fast. Nick smelled the booze.

"Your father doesn't want us around anymore," his mother said finally, looking straight ahead over the steering wheel. "He's divorcing me, and he doesn't want you, either."

The Dead Woman in His Room

After a long pause she said: "You know what he said about you and your sister? Your father, Mr. Respectability. The big 'Hi, I'm Nick Barons.' You want to know what he said about you and your sister Elizabeth?"

Nick's mother turned toward him abruptly and grabbed his leg, hard, with her right hand. "He said, 'And take those beaner kids with you!' That's what he said." The car veered wildly when his mother jerked herself back in front of the steering wheel.

Nick was scared. He didn't know what a beaner kid was.

He found out on the first day at his new school in Denver. Colfax Junior High was a large public school that drew kids from the north and west side of town. There were some genuinely "integrated" neighborhoods in this area, but, for the most part, it was divided into neighborhoods that were segmented by race. African Americans lived in one section, Chicanos in another, Asians in a third. American Indians, for the most part, lived in the barrio with the Chicanos. There was very little cross over. If you showed up in a neighborhood that didn't match your race, you were noticed. Each ethnic group had a slur associated with it. Chicanos were "beaners."

The school system operated on the pretense that all races were equal, but the reality was that all races were separate. It had been that way for long enough that inertia made it seem somehow natural and right. School administrators may not have consciously placed kids on the basis of race, but most classes reflected the same divisions as the neighborhoods.

Nick's new address in Denver, put him in classes where English was a second language for a lot of the students who had grown up speaking Spanish. Nick, Jr. didn't speak Spanish. His mother had insisted he only speak English. It had been her dream all her life to get out of the barrio, and she didn't want to hear the sound of it coming from her own children.

Nick didn't speak at all for two days. On the third day, at recess, he was beaten by a group of white kids who felt he was intruding on their part of the school yard. He sat that afternoon in class with a split lip and a bruise spreading across the left side of his face; and said nothing. His teacher made a note to keep an eye on him. He could be a troublemaker.

Growing up in South Winds, Nick Jr. was very used to being alone. That ability served him well during what remained of his time in seventh grade. He started to learn to speak Spanish that summer, but he would never be able to speak without an accent. He'd spoken English too long. Even his name didn't fit. A Chicano kid named Nick Barons, Jr. Later, when he could have changed his name, he kept it deliberately. He thought of his father every time someone called him by name, and it fanned the anger. The anger was who he became.

By the time he reached high school, there was very little left of the kid from South Winds who grew up exploring a backyard that seemed to go on forever. This other Nick, Jr. lived in a crowded apartment in the barrio with his mother and sister. His mother had deteriorated rapidly after the divorce. She certainly wasn't the beautiful dark-haired model that Nick Barons had married. She'd put on weight, and, to her horror, she had begun to look increasingly like the exhausted Chicano women around her; women like her own mother.

One of the insidious cruelties of the white racism embedded in American culture is that it usurps the healthy self-image of Chicanos and other minority groups and replaces it in their minds with the prejudicial image of the racist. They see themselves as the racists see them. It is the ultimate identity theft.

Nick's mother got next to nothing in the divorce settlement. According to all the records available to the court, Nick Sr. appeared to be on the verge of bankruptcy. Everything he owned was mortgaged to the hilt. She got $550 a month in alimony, and her attorney told her to take it.

The Dead Woman in His Room

She still had the prescriptions for Valium from the doctor Nick had found for her, and she re-filled them often. Her other drug was her hatred for her husband; and she never ran out of it; even after she read in the *Rocky Mountain News* that he had been found dead at a hunting lodge in the foothills west of Boulder. She may have hated him even more after that. The alimony stopped.

Nick's sister Elizabeth was assimilated into the barrio with much less resistance. She had her mother's natural beauty without her mother's aversion to everything Chicano. She didn't live to get out of the barrio. She didn't really seem to live until she got into the barrio. She learned to speak Spanish easily. She made friends, and, by the time, she was 12, it was hard to imagine that she had ever lived anywhere else. She took the nickname EB.

EB was a gang banger. It was EB who got Nick recruited for *Los Vientos* (The Winds). He was 16. There were several who didn't want him in the gang because of his reputation as a loner. He would have to prove himself.

That's when Nick went back to South Winds. It was the first time he'd been there since the day his mother drove them to their new home in north Denver. Nick planned to break into the house where he once lived, but there was a party going on at his old house, and the place was lit up and noisy. He left the car he had stolen in Denver in his old driveway where it wouldn't be noticed with all the others. Then he set out on foot across the sage and pine-covered hill that separated this ranchette from the one next door. It was dark, but he knew the way.

He'd been in this house before it was built. The contractors had befriended him and taken him all through it during different stages in its construction. He remembered some happy afternoons sitting in the hot sun on stacks of lumber with the men, pretending he was one of them; before his mother made him stay away. She didn't want him associating with workers.

After the house was built and the Haskells moved in, Nick had been inside a few times, but he never became friends with the

The Dead Woman in His Room

Haskell boy who was a year older than him. Teddy, he'd almost forgotten his name was Teddy. Teddy and his father Freddy. He had once envied their closeness before he knew what envy really was. Teddy was away at boarding school now. Nick couldn't remember the mother's name. She didn't like him; he could tell. Even then, he had a sense that he wasn't acceptable somehow.

Nick let himself in through a basement door. It wasn't locked. The residents of South Winds were mostly convinced they were far enough from the city to be safe from people like him. He figured the Haskells would be at the party. There were no lights on in the house. It was dark, but the moonlight that came through the picture windows was enough for him to get around inside without a problem. Nick was not new to burglary.

Nick stood for a few moments in the living room to get his bearings. Then he went upstairs. It was very quiet. He stood for a while at the doorway to Teddy's room. And then moved down the hall. The master bedroom occupied the entire west side of the second floor with French doors that opened onto a deck.

There were expensive things everywhere, but he went directly to the dressing room to look for jewelry. It was darker here, away from the windows. He stood for a while to let his eyes adjust to this deeper darkness. Then he looked for something to take; something that would prove what he'd done; that he hadn't just stolen from some other poor Chicano family in the barrio; that he had left the barrio and stolen from the other world: from the rich white world, far away. He studied the shelves around the makeup mirror, looking for a jewelry box.

Standing there in the dark, another image came to mind. It was the image of his mother sitting in front of her makeup mirror in her dressing room. It was only a week before they had left the house. His mother sat on a stool in front of the lighted mirror, combing her long black hair. There was a water glass on the dresser half filled with straight Bourbon. She drank from it occasionally, as if it were some distasteful medicine she had to finish. She was preparing for bed. An empty bed. At this point, Nick's father rarely slept at the house. At least the shouting had stopped.

His mother would sometimes sit at her dressing table for hours at the end of the day, brushing out her long black hair in front of the mirror. Nick knew not to disturb her. This night the door was ajar, and, in his memory, Nick could see his mother through the opening. She had on a short pink satin wrap that was loosely tied. He could see the shape of her breast through the shear material, and he realized, if he looked beyond her into the mirror, he could see her breasts almost totally uncovered from the front. As his mother brushed her hair, her wrap opened and closed with each motion of her arm, closing a little less each time. The nipple of her left breast was almost uncovered, and he became mesmerized by the slow incremental opening of her wrap as his mother continued her methodical brushing. At one point his mother stopped brushing her hair and sat up very straight and leaned forward. He could no longer see her image in her mirror. Then she set her brush down and took a long drink from the water glass of Bourbon. When she leaned back to her original position, she slid her hand inside her wrap and began fondling her breast, the left breast, the one he had almost seen. She closed her eyes and gently massaged her breast so that the nipple moved up and down. He stood in the dark watching, almost holding his breath. He knew she had seen him.

"Beth," he heard.

Then, right behind him. "What time is it, Beth? I must have fallen asleep."

The overhead light came on as Nick turned toward the voice. Freddy Haskell was standing in the doorway in tennis shorts and a wrinkled polo shirt. He held his right hand up to his face. He was yawning. His hair was all pushed to one side. He had athletic socks on his feet. They had a thin line of red stitching near the top.

The Dead Woman in His Room

Freddy Haskell looked at Nick for a long moment. Then he said, "Who are you? Did Beth send you? What are you doing in here?" Freddy Haskell was waking up by stages. "Are you a friend of Teddy's? Is Teddy here?" He looked more closely at Nick. Then he said, "You don't belong here. I don't know you. I'm calling the cops." Freddy Haskell turned his back to leave the room.

"Don't move," Nick said.

Freddy Haskell turned back toward Nick. He was taller than Nick and broader. "So, you speak English. Great. Well listen to this: This is my house. You can't tell me what to do in my house." He looked at Nick again. "I don't know what you're doing here. You don't belong here. If you don't leave right now, I'm going to call the cops."

Freddy Haskell prided himself on being in charge. That's how he ran his company. That's how he ran his family. He gave orders. Everyone obeyed. He was the boss. He was the husband. He was the father. He was the captain of the team. He was always in charge. It was his right. It always had been. He stared at Nick.

"I know you," Freddy Haskell said. "You're that Barons kid, aren't you? I remember you."

Nick looked at him. He didn't move. He didn't speak.

"What's wrong with you? Are you on drugs? Answer me." Freddy Haskell glowered. He stepped closer.

When Nick hit Freddy Haskell in the face with his fist, Haskell's socks slipped on the polished tile floor, and he fell backwards into the darkness in the hallway. No one ever hit Freddy Haskell.

Lying on his back in the hallway, Freddy Haskell looked up in amazement at Nick who was now silhouetted in the doorway, standing over him. He saw Nick pull something out of his right front pocket. Then he heard the blade of the knife snap out of the grip held loosely in Nick's right hand.

Still on his back on the floor Freddy Haskell scrambled backwards on his hands and heels. The friction against the hall carpet pulled his tennis shorts down. When he rolled over to get up, his naked white ass was hanging out of his white shorts.

Nick kicked him and sent him sprawling down the hall. Freddy Haskell landed on his stomach. His white tennis shorts were now down around his thighs. It made it hard for him to stand up. He twisted on the floor, grabbing at his pants.

"What are you doing? What do you want? Why are you doing this?"

Nick heard the fear. He liked it. He let Freddy Haskell get up on his knees and pull his pants up. Then he kicked him in the face, not too hard. Freddy Haskell landed on his side. He pushed himself up immediately. His lip was bleeding.

"I have money," he said. "Cash. Lots of it. I'll tell you where it is. You can have it. Just let me get up. I'll show you." Freddy Haskell got his feet under him as Nick slowly approached. He was under a skylight in front of Teddy's room where Nick could see him better. His nose was running into the blood from his split lip. He was breathing harder now.

Nick didn't seem to be breathing at all. He was watching himself. He was realizing things about himself. He was thinking. He was thinking about his father.

Freddy Haskell sprang. Tennis had kept him in good shape and college football had taught him how to tackle someone hard. He hit Nick just below the ribs. The force of it carried Nick backwards down the hall. He landed on his back with Freddy Haskell on top of him. Haskell outweighed him by almost eighty pounds. Nick gulped for breath and Haskell got up first.

"You fucking little beaner punk! Break into my house!" He picked up Nick's knife where it had fallen. "Get the fuck out of here."

Nick got up.

"You better get out of here. I've got your knife," Freddy Haskell said.

Nick smiled.

"I'm telling you. You better get out of here. Get out now, and I won't even call the cops," Freddy Haskell said. "Just get out of here."

Nick kept smiling. He had another knife.

~~~

After Nick killed Freddy Haskell, he walked back to the dressing room that he now knew belonged to Beth. He selected a jewelry box with an inscription on it and dumped a pearl necklace out onto the floor. Later that night, back in the barrio, he presented an exquisite mahogany jewelry box to the leaders of *Los Vientos*. Inside was most of the right ear of Freddy Haskell.

~~~

Nick didn't stay in Denver after that. He didn't become a member of *Los Vientos*. Instead, he left the next day for Los Angeles. By the time he was 19, he was sent to prison for armed assault. By the time he got out, he was 27 and a member of the *Norteños*, a Chicano gang that started in the prison system in LA and had grown into a loosely affiliated national organization of gangs around the country.

Nick was still a loner. Leaders of different gangs who needed to make an example of somebody hired him for the job rather than expose their members to the risk of getting caught. Having no connections anywhere made Nick almost invisible. Mostly, Nick killed white guys—businessmen, like his father. He liked to watch them die. He'd gotten very good at what he did. He always used a knife. It made it personal. He liked seeing that moment when his victims knew they were dying and were helpless to do anything about it. He liked being the last one they saw. It was like sending a message to his father.

Nick had no permanent home. He lived where his next job was. And when it was done, he lived somewhere else. He had a territory like a traveling salesman that included LA, Las Vegas, Reno, Denver and as far east as Chicago and Detroit.

The Dead Woman in His Room

He was in Denver briefly when his sister was killed. She'd been shot off her motorcycle early one morning on a ride back from Boulder. Shot like a deer in a field. It made him crazy that no one knew who the shooter had been. Like his father, he couldn't kill him either.

His mother's killer was less random. She was dying of diabetes. She'd already lost a leg and was restricted to her room in the small house Nick bought for her in north Denver. She wouldn't go to Elizabeth's funeral. She had no sympathy to share for anyone but herself. She had no friends. Nick hired nurses for her, but they all spoke Spanish. And she still only spoke English. Mostly she lived on downers and beer and the embers of her hatred for what Nick's father had done to her.

Nick thought of his father every time he killed some other white guy for the *Norteños*. The killing itself wasn't that big a deal for Nick, Jr. at this point. Thinking that he was killing his father made it more satisfying. If he had actually killed his father, he could have only done it once. Once would not be enough.

Nick found some other white guy to kill when his mother died, and he went to Denver for her funeral. In his mother's possessions was a stack of papers that had belonged to his father. Among them was a detailed account of the money Nick deposited in HAL Holdings, an offshore bank. Made stupid by the drugs and blind by her hatred, Nick's mother never realized what the papers meant.

But Nick did. As he sat in the living room of his dead mother's house he realized this was money that should have belonged to him and his mother and sister. This offshore bank was why his father was able to appear almost insolvent in divorce court. He converted all his assets to cash and diverted the cash to HAL Holdings. $2.3 million had been deposited in total. This was his money. Stolen by his father.

He had no idea how his mother got this information. She obviously had no idea what it was. Nick knew. He knew about offshore accounts. He knew that money could still be there. The last two pages in the stack of papers were a handwritten diary of Nick's meetings with somebody named Kyle Leary. Now he had two names: HAL Holdings and Kyle Leary. This was some part of his father that wasn't dead yet.

Nick was too young to understand what had happened when he and his mother and sister were tossed like trash into the barrio by his father. Standing in his dead mother's living room, he understood. They were robbed.

Three years later, Kyle is dead, and the woman; but he still hasn't found HAL Holdings. The only link left is the old guy in the High Rise, and his nephew. All his anger transfers to them.

9

"Anything you haven't done yet, Bud?"

Soon after Pete showed up in Mill River to look after his uncle Willie, he started taking small groups of High Rise residents on short trips in his van, usually running errands of some kind. Very few residents of the High Rise had cars, so driving people around town was a good way to get to know them. Besides, Willie liked riding in Pete's van and running errands with and for other High Rise residents gave them a purpose for their rides. Occasionally, they took field trips to a variety of destinations and events around Mill River.

Today's field trip to the 300-acre Sky Meadow Wildlife Farm is their most adventurous to date. Pete decided to go ahead with it even after finding the dead woman in his room. The police kept him overnight. But they let him go in the morning. They didn't have enough evidence to hold him, as much as officer Henderson wanted to. That was Friday. Today is Sunday and Pete wants to put the whole thing behind him. He gave everyone who had originally wanted to go on the field trip the option to back out, but everyone still wants to go; not that all of them are that conscious of their choices.

Hilary and Rose, for example are two developmentally impaired sisters in their early 40s. They have the mental capacity of about seven and nine, respectively. Rose claims she can read, but she always demonstrates this ability with the same book: *The*

The Dead Woman in His Room

Cat in The Hat, by Dr. Seuss. The book was a gift from their mother who had her daughters placed in a group home shortly before she died of colon cancer six years ago. Hilary and Rose had done so well in the group home that they moved two years ago into their own apartment in the High Rise. They are very proud of their independence. Rose does all the cooking. Mostly they live on cold cereal and TV dinners heated in the microwave. They are a little afraid of the stove. Hilary and Rose have no idea that a dead woman was found in Pete's room.

Nor, as far as anyone could tell, does Gretchen. Gretchen is a 75-year old schizophrenic whom Foxy had finagled an apartment for in the High Rise. Horribly abused as a child, Gretchen spent most of her life in a state mental hospital. When the state closed the mental hospitals, Gretchen was supposedly "re-integrated into mainstream society" which meant, in reality, that she joined the ranks of the chronically insane living on the streets. Gretchen came for some of her meals to the shelter that Foxy helped run in Mill River, but she wouldn't stay overnight. The barracks in the shelter reminded her too much of the mental hospital. As badly as she fared on the streets, she feared nothing more than being sent back to the mental hospital. The state closed the mental hospitals years ago, but they were still very much open in Gretchen's mind.

With some creative pulling of administrative strings and some artful dodging on medical forms, Foxy managed to get Gretchen into a studio apartment in the High Rise, and, with the support of two matronly widows, Marge Malone and Anna Gutowski, Gretchen settled in…mostly. She is still nuts. She often wears an American Flag wrapped around her head and most days she walks the streets talking to unseen companions. But, for the last two years, at least, she finds her way back to her little apartment in the High Rise most nights. Marge and Anna accepted Gretchen for who she was and, maybe because of their acceptance,

The Dead Woman in His Room

Gretchen seemed to become less crazy. She was also eating better. Marge and Anna love to cook. Especially Anna.

Marge and Anna are in their late 60s and usually dress in sweatpants and sneakers. When they sit together, as they often do at one of the picnic tables on the grounds of the High Rise, they look a little like two well-scrubbed potatoes. They knew each other before moving into the High Rise but didn't become friends until they became next-door neighbors on the third floor. Anna has the apartment next to Marge's but seems to spend most of her time in Marge's apartment. They have both been on their own for years.

Marge's husband died in a construction accident 20 years ago. He was standing in the wrong place when a chain, that was being used to pull a backhoe out of the mud broke, snapped back and crushed his skull. There was a big funeral. He was very well liked in town.

Anna's husband abandoned her when their son was six. When her son grew up he was sent to Vietnam. Shortly after he returned he OD'd on drugs in her garage. He was 20.

Marge's son Patrick is a patrol cop with the Mill River Police Department. He comes every Sunday to visit his mother at the High Rise. Two Christmases ago he gave Marge a police band radio-scanner so she could listen to the patrol cars talking back and forth with headquarters. It quickly became her prize possession and the centerpiece of her day. The police scanner was such a good present that the next Christmas Marge's son gave his mother and her friend Anna a set of two bright yellow walkie-talkies. Marge and Anna take them everywhere. They're tucked in the beach bag they are bringing with them on this field trip. They don't trust cell phones.

The only one of the original group who dropped out of the trip to the petting zoo is Ralph. His decision not to go has nothing to do with the dead woman in Pete's apartment. Ralph Berge is an intelligent, distinguished-looking man in his late 60s. For all outward appearances, he looks like a respectable retiree who would seem more at home in faculty lounge than a subsidized housing facility. Ralph's sophisticated air, however, masks a history of violent bi-polar swings that cost him his career, his money, and his family.

Ralph takes a perverse satisfaction in the totality of his personal failure. It's his singular accomplishment. At his prime, Ralph was a tenured professor of philosophy at a private liberal arts college. Over time, a gap appeared between the rhetoric of the philosophers whose writings he expounded and the reality of the world he lived and saw around him. Gradually, the gap tore through his intellect, eventually separating it almost entirely from his emotional self.

Ralph has a problem with Lithium, the current drug of choice for manic depressives, so he's given Thorazine to subdue his emotional swings. Thorazine keeps Ralph's manic episodes at bay, more or less, but it has several unfortunate side effects. One of the most awkward for Ralph is the way it causes his arms to float up from his sides involuntarily when he's stressed. Like a lot of manic depressives, Ralph is capable of very clear insight into the mental condition of other residents, but, with few exceptions, he practices this ability with restraint. He doesn't use it to build relationships, nor is he mean. He just sees without touching. He also avoids being touched.

Ralph has the apartment next to Willie's on the 5th floor. He's been there for about four years, and in that time, he's left the grounds of the High Rise only for doctor's appointments in the hospital about a quarter of a mile away. He always takes a cab, and he always asks for the same driver. It was a surprise when Ralph said he would go on the field trip. It was less of a surprise when he backed out.

Ralph called Bud Buchard, the neighbor on the other side of Willie, to tell him that he didn't feel well and would stay home. Bud knew Ralph well enough to accept his excuse; although he knew it wasn't true. Bud actually understood Ralph better than Ralph understood Bud. Why Bud's blindness interfered with Ralph's clairvoyance was unclear, but it seemed to.

Bud and Ralph were very different people. Ralph's world had been the contemplative grounds of the Ivy League. Bud was born in Trinidad, grew up in foster homes, and spent most of his life on the deck of ships as a seaman in the merchant marine. While Ralph was working on his homonyms at a private middle school in Andover, Massachusetts, Bud was a cook on container ships hauling freight between California and Asian ports of call.

Bud got US citizenship by serving in the U.S. Navy during the Vietnam War. He left the navy after the second time he was wounded and went on to spend his whole working life on board ship. By the time he retired, he was already starting to go blind. With his characteristically dry wit, Bud said he never wanted to see the sea again anyway. Bud came to Mill River to live with his sister, a retired schoolteacher who, like Bud, had never married. He moved into the High Rise after his sister died.

Bud has a sailor's fatalism about the things that happen in a person's life. Unlike Ralph, he isn't tormented either by a need to accomplish something important or by the need to understand. "You have to deal with what you get," he told Pete in an understated philosophical exchange.

With Bud, what you see is pretty much what you get. He's tall and dark, with grey hair and a kind smile. He has the bearing of someone who has served in the military, but a gentleness appears on second glance that suggests he has spent more time puzzling about life than imposing himself on it.

Bud walks the streets of Mill River incessantly. The weather never deters him. He goes out in the worst weather, dressed in a bright yellow slicker with a rain hat pulled low over his face, walking with his long white cane. Chick-zzzzt...Chick-zzzzt...Chick-zzzzt...Chick-zzzzt. Wherever he goes, the sound of the metal tip on his cane hitting and sliding on the ground always proceeds him. He walks surprisingly fast, without any hesitation.

Bud helped Willie when he couldn't find his apartment shortly after moving into the High Rise, and they soon became friends. Increasingly, Willie thinks Bud plays stand-up bass in his jazz band. He doesn't.

As different as they each are, Willie, Ralph and Bud are good neighbors and, in their own ways, good friends. They walk the quarter mile trail around the grounds several times a day, and the Chick-zzzzt…Chick-zzzzt…Chick-zzzzt…of Bud's cane is a familiar sound to the other residents. Over time Willie contributes less and less to their conversations. At first, they are comfortable enough with each other not to find Willie's silence inappropriate. Reluctantly they have come to admit that Willie's mind is failing him. Watching Willie slip away draws Ralph and Bud closer together. When Pete shows up at the High Rise, he joins them on their walks. Eventually, Pete takes on greater responsibility for Willie, but he does it in a way that includes Ralph and Bud. He has that knack.

This morning, Pete has the van warmed up and idling in the corner of the parking lot where they are to meet. It's a two-hour drive to the petting zoo, and they all agreed to leave by 9. Hilary and Rose aren't very good about being on time, and Foxy has gone to fetch them. Marge and Anna are sitting at the picnic table nearby, sorting out the various food containers they have brought along for the trip. No one is going to go hungry while these two are in charge of the food. Gretchen is watching them. Gretchen is a little uneasy about the prospect of riding in the van, but she trusts Marge and Anna, and she adores Pete. Gretchen generally avoids men but when, on a hunch, Pete gave her a big box of colored pencils and several sketch books, it opened a kind of communication between them. Gretchen keeps her art supplies in a canvas book bag she carries everywhere. Pete gave her the book bag, too. Her sketches are primitive but have a haunting quality about them that makes it obvious they are not the drawings of a child.

Pete hoped that Foxy would ride up front with him on this trip, but Willie has made it very clear that his claim on riding shotgun is inviolate. He isn't taking any chances and is already sitting in his seat in the van. Pete knows that people with Alzheimer sometimes come across as passive aggressive. He suspects Willie of covering one with the other on more than one occasion. But there is nothing to be gained by arguing with him.

Pete and Bud are standing between the van and the picnic table talking about Ralph's decision not to come along.

"You don't think he'd do anything to himself, do you?" Pete asks Bud.

"You mean like kill himself."

"Well, yeah. Like that. He's not suicidal, is he?"

"No. I don't think so." Bud tapes his cane a few times, as if grounding himself. "I knew a guy who killed himself. This guy wasn't like Ralph at all. It was during the Vietnam War. We'd been on leave in Da Nang and this guy just didn't want to go back into combat. It didn't make sense to me. I was trying my best not to get shot. We only had a month to go. He died. I didn't."

"Anything you haven't done yet, Bud?" Pete asks.

"Yeah," Bud says. He taps his cane a couple more times, turns toward Pete and smiles. "Guess that's why I'm not suicidal."

They both laugh.

"I was wondering," Bud says. "Now that Ralph isn't going, maybe Slate, you know, that kid who hangs around here sometimes, maybe he could go with us."

"Yeah, I know Slate, but I haven't seen him. I don't know if he's around today."

"He's over by the front door."

Pete looks, and Slate is there. "How did you know he was there? I didn't see him, and I'm not blind."

The Dead Woman in His Room

"Well, it's a good thing," Bud says. "You're the one driving today, aren't you?"

Pete laughs. "Really. How did you know he was there?"

"Funny thing I've learned about being blind is that sometimes I'm aware of things that other people can't see. Besides, I knew kids like that back in the orphanage."

"You were in an orphanage? I didn't know that."

"Me and my sister ... in New Orleans. Not one of my favorite stories."

"I can imagine." Pete says. "Let's ask Slate if he wants to come along. It's fine with me. Walk over with me," Pete adds. "You can point him out."

Slate is small for his age. He has long dark hair that his mother cuts for him and big brown eyes. Slate is a little like the Cheshire cat in *Alice in Wonderland*. He has the ability to make himself invisible to most adults, even most kids. Bud is one of few people who is always aware of Slate when he comes around to visit his grandmother in the High Rise. Bud seems to have a kind of radar that lets him know whenever someone is nearby. Bud's radar doesn't just pick up Slate, but the fact that Slate is noticed by Bud is of particular significance to the boy. People who can actually see Slate often don't notice him, but Slate could be at his most invisible, and Bud would know he was there. Slate had tested it. Gradually, without anyone else noticing, the boy no one noticed became friends with the man who couldn't see.

Slate came to the High Rise most afternoons. His grandmother Gladys is just under 5 feet and just over 450 pounds. She hasn't left her apartment in two years. Slate runs errands for her and, although it's against the rules of the High Rise, he sometimes stays overnight. Slate's mother Sam— Gladys' only child—lives with her boyfriend Wayne in a duplex across town. Periodically, Sam goes to the safe house to get away from Wayne's abuse. When Sam is in the safe-house, Slate stays with her grandmother. Slate has lately been staying more often with his grandmother.

Bud calls Gladys from the phone in the lobby and gets permission for Slate to come on the field trip. By that time, Foxy has arrived with Hilary and Rose, everyone clambers into the back of the van, and Pete slides the door shut. Marge, Gretchen, and Anna are in the first row in the back. Slate and Bud sit in the second row—the narrow seat, and Hilary, Rose and Foxy sit in the last row. When Pete jumps into the driver's seat across from Willie it's 9:30 am, and the day is already warming up.

"To the zoo," Pete says, ceremoniously dropping the van into Drive and pulling out of the High Rise parking lot. Everyone is caught up with buckling their seatbelts and becoming aware of each other in the van. Spirits are high. It's exciting to be going somewhere together.

Only Willie turns to look back as they drive away. He leans against the window squinting at something he's seen. He looks for a long time.

"I think I saw Nick Barons," he says, turning toward Pete who is still settling into his seat for the drive, adjusting his shoulders.

"Yeah. Who's Nick Barons?" Pete asks without looking over.

Willie starts to answer and then just exhales. "I don't know. Somebody."

"Yeah, probably," Pete says. "Well, there's no more room on this bus. He'll have to take the next one."

Willie shrugs and looks ahead. Most of the time he likes riding in the front seat of Pete's van.

~ ~ ~

In the back, after helping Hilary and Rose find their respective seatbelts and snapping them in, Foxy realizes how long it has been since she was a passenger in someone else's car. It's been so long she almost forgot why she never rides as a passenger in someone else's car. She feels the familiar stirrings of panic rising from deep within her and reaches in her purse for a small blue plastic pill box. She fingers two pills briefly and then discreetly tucks one under her tongue. Then she takes a deep breath and looks across the seats in front of her through the windshield. Pete catches her eye in the rear-view mirror. She smiles, but the tension has already made her face feel like a mask. It's going to be a very long ride. Being a passenger in a car always brings back memories.

It was a very long time ago. They were returning from a medical conference outside of London; two aspiring young doctors serving their internships in the Priory Hospital in Roehampton, one of the leading private psychiatric hospitals in the UK. They had met and fallen in love at Kings College London. They were both scholarship students, and the top two students in their class. Rising out of a tunnel of 18-hour days of study for six years and 20-hour days as interns, they were about to embark on careers that promised to take them wherever they wanted to go. And they wanted to go there together: Siobhan (Foxy) McFarlane, the redheaded Irish girl from County Donegal, Ireland and Desmond King, a black man from Port of Spain, Trinidad.

Their small convertible car was hit on the driver's side by a lorry rushing fresh produce to market. Desmond was killed instantly. When the little car stopped flipping across the intersection it landed upside down. Foxy was trapped under the car with her head pressed hard between the bonnet and the road. The luggage rack saved her life. Every time the people at the scene tried to lift the car, it settled back squeezing her head harder into the road. She heard them talking. She could see their shoes under the upside down car. She could see the lights reflecting in what she thought was rain on the road. She didn't remember it raining. She remembered screaming.

Two days later she woke up in a hospital room. Her parents were there. They told her that Desmond was in another room. They didn't tell her he was dead. They said she was going to be all right. That wasn't true, either. She was physically okay. She had a badly broken arm, and she'd lost a lot of blood. The right side of her face was scraped and laced with shallow cuts where the road had touched her almost gently as the car slid to a stop. But those wounds healed. Her sense of her life, of who she was and where she was going, was shattered.

Sitting in the back of Pete's van on the way to the wild animal petting zoo, she is forced again to accept that pieces of her life are still missing. She never completed her internship and never practiced as a doctor. She took a job as a waitress in London. After that job, she took another job, and then another; drifting across Europe; finally wandering as far as the United States. She often looked back through all those jobs for the person she had been, but she never found her.

The sound of Rose giggling brings her back to the present. Rose is wiggling in her seat and has her hand over her mouth. She points to her sister.

"Hilary has to go pee-pee," she says, laughing outright now. "Hilary has to go pee-pee."

They were twenty minutes into the trip.

~~~

The two-hour trip took about three hours with all the stops. Rose insisted she didn't have to go to the bathroom when they stopped at the first mini-market, but less than twenty minutes later, it was Hilary's turn to announce in a fit of giggles that "Rose has to go pee-pee."

Pete doesn't mind stopping. They are passing through several towns on a state road heading into the Berkshires, and they are never far from a place to stop. Bud and Slate buy coffee for everyone at the next mini market. Bud pours, and Slate puts the tops on and sticks the cups in the carboard trays.

On the way out, Pete sees a pair of sunglasses like Bud's on a rack and buys a pair for Slate. Slate emerges from the store carrying the tray of coffee cups, sporting his new pair of dark glasses and almost falls off the front step. He's never had a pair of dark glasses before. Back in the van Slate looks at his reflection in the window and admires his glasses. He said he wanted coffee, but Bud bought him a chocolate milk and poured it into a coffee cup with a lid like the others had. In his seat Slate closes his eyes and keeps them closed for a long time turning his head to see what it feels like to look and not be able to see.

Willie is the next one to have to stop. Coffee goes right through Willie. This stop is a gas station, and, while Willie goes to the men's room, Pete fills up the van with gas. Foxy is the only other one who gets out. She's taking deep breaths.

"It's nice up here in the hills, isn't it," Pete says.

Foxy looks at him, "What?"

"The air, you know, mountain air, away from the city, makes you want to take deep breaths."

"Oh. Yeah," she smiles, stiffly.

Pete looks at the gas nozzle for a while.

"You okay?" he asks.

"Yeah," she says too quickly. "Yeah I'm fine. Just a little car sick. You know riding in the back and all. I'm not used to it."

"I was going to say you could ride up front, but Willie won't give up that seat for anything."

"Yeah. I can tell. I'll be all right. Really."

Pete tops off the gas tank a couple of times and hangs the nozzle on the pump.

"You want to drive for a while? You can if you want."

Foxy looks surprised. But her face relaxes a little. "You wouldn't mind? You sure?"

"Hey. We can switch off." He shrugs his shoulders. "We're stopping every 20 minutes anyway."

Foxy laughs.

"You know how to drive this thing? It's big, and it's ugly, but it is automatic."

"No problem. I can drive anything."

"I figured." He holds out the keys.

The Dead Woman in His Room

Foxy looks up at him as she takes them from his hand. "Thanks. I appreciate it."

"Hey. I wanted to sit next to Rose, anyway," Pete says. He shuffles his feet and looks toward the gas station. "Here's Willie now. Let's see how far we get before our next rest stop."

Pete climbs in the back and slides the door closed. Foxy hears Hilary and Rose laughing as she walks around to the driver's door.

Willie looks at Foxy curiously when she gets behind the wheel and pulls the driver's seat forward. "Hey Willie," Pete calls from the back. "Foxy's going to drive for a while. That okay with you?"

"Okay," Willie says looking straight ahead. He seems distracted after coming back to the van. He looks out the side window and then back at Foxy. "I think I saw Nick Barons," he says to her matter-of-factly.

Foxy is adjusting the mirrors and settling into the seat. "Oh. Who's that Willie?"

"I can't remember. Somebody I knew, I guess."

"Where did you see him last?" Foxy asks, watching for traffic as she pulls out onto the state road.

"I saw him before."

"Before what Willie?"

"I'm not sure," Willie says, looking out the side window. "But I think I just saw him again."

10

"Everyone choose a buddy."

It's after noon by the time they pull into the parking lot at the Sky Meadow Wildlife Farm. The farm is a popular local attraction. Situated on several hundred acres in the hills above the Hudson River valley, it consists of a series of 5- to 10-acre fenced-in fields that are shared by different kinds of domestic and wild animals. There are goats in with llamas and antelopes in with deer and elk. There are horses and mules and burros and hogs and cattle in all shapes and sizes. The buffalo family of four has the largest field to itself. Emus wander around in several of the fields, but the ostriches have their own area. There are no rides, and no concessions. Foot trails connect all the fields, so people can walk between them. There is also a gravel road, so visitors can drive through the entire complex. Most of the visitors are school groups or parents with small children, but there are also quite a number of elderly visitors driven through the park by their children and grandchildren. Pete found the zoo on one of his longer drives with Willie. They hadn't stopped then, but Pete thought it would be a good place to take a group from the High Rise someday.

It's a warm day for late September, and they decide to have a picnic lunch before entering the park. The parking lot is crowded, but Foxy is able to find a place to park among the mini vans and SUVs, not very far from the picnic grounds. Pete's van stands out from the other cars in the lot. It's almost 20 years old, and the last two coats of paint – one blue and one white – are mottled with blotches of rust that give the overall van a kind of tie-dyed look from a distance. Up close, it looks as if the body would skid off the frame if it stopped too quickly or hit a bad bump on a corner. Mechanically, it's in good shape, and it has good tires, but aesthetically it says aging hippie and/or migrant worker, depending on what part of the country it's passing through. Usually Pete has it rigged out as a camper, but he outfitted it with seats shortly after coming to Mill River. It makes a good tour bus for people who aren't self-conscious about what they show up in.

Everyone in the van this day is feeling pretty good. Foxy is glad she didn't take the second Xanax at the beginning of the trip and is clear headed enough to drive safely. Concentrating on the drive and feeling in control erased all but a residue of panic from her system. She still feels that. But she also feels the hail-fellow-well-met camaraderie that the van trip has brought out in everyone. Hilary and Rose demonstrate all the enthusiasm of their intellectual age and are giggling and pointing and pressing their faces against the window as Foxy negotiates the parking lot. Slate, the one actual child in the group, is taking his cues from Bud; their heads moving slightly from side to side with their matching sunglasses on.

After Foxy gets the van parked, Pete slides the side door open and, after stretching and looking around at their new surroundings, everyone joins him at the back of the van to carry the cardboard boxes they are using as picnic baskets to their table. Foxy and Willie lead the way. There is one large beat-up red cooler that Pete carries, following the rest of them as they work their way through the picnic area in search of an open table. Most of the tables are occupied, and they have to twist and turn around people and picnic gear and several jogging strollers on their way to an open table.

The Dead Woman in His Room

Because he's following everyone else, Pete becomes aware of the reaction that his little band of travelers is getting from the gathering of fellow picnickers. It's subtle, at first: a few heads turn. Then there's some pointing. Foxy and Willie pass without much notice; and Marge and Anna. But Gretchen gets people looking. She's tall and walks very erect, and she's dressed in multi-colored layers, the uniform of the homeless. Around her head she wears what most second glances reveal as a slightly soiled American flag, pinned in the back with a long turquoise barrette. By the time the second glance reveals the nature of Gretchen's head gear, the sound of Gretchen's animated, if one-sided conversation confirms the suspicion in most observers that there is something very different about Gretchen. If she's nervous at all, Gretchen talks to people who aren't there, an affectation that often unnerves the people who are there. If she becomes agitated, her side of the conversation can become heated, complete with gestures that support whatever unknown point she happens to be making to her unseen conversationalists. There is usually more than one. Gretchen has been quiet on the ride, and she isn't nervous yet, but the potential is there.

Next in the procession are Bud and Slate. With his dark glasses on and the way he copies Bud's slightly robotic gait, Slate appears to be the blind child leading the blind man. This image is at least non-threatening, but it does contribute to the weird band-of-gypsies appearance of the group.

Hilary and Rose are showstoppers. They're having a ball and are completely unselfconscious in their enthusiasm for this place and all these people. Dressed in matching jogging outfits, they look from a distance like the 40-something women they are. Their movements, however, are much more like those of young children. They also have the big round heads and bemused expressions that broadcast "developmentally impaired." They laugh and giggle and point and smile at everyone and everything.

Not everyone smiles back. Occupied with following Foxy and carrying their packages, no one else in the group seems to notice the young mother who snatches her toddler up as if out of harm's way when Gretchen walks by; or the two seven year old girls who mock the exaggerated gestures of Hilary and Rose; or the two boys about the same age who bumped into each other as if they were blind and fall down laughing, and then get up and do it over and over again. Pete notices. It's a new experience for him. He's never felt so protective of a group of people before. With the extended self-consciousness of a new parent, he sees every guarded look, feels every implied slight. He takes it all very personally. He's bristling by the time he gets to the picnic table and, after setting the cooler down he turns around and glowers at the other picnickers.

Foxy hands him a paper plate with a fat turkey sandwich and a mound of Anna's homemade potato salad. "Want some coffee with that?" she says. When Pete turns back to the table, he sees everyone looking up at him attentively as if they are waiting for him to say something.

"Let's eat," he says after a pause. "Looks like we've got a lot of animals to pet." Pete sits down at the end of the table. Willie is on his right and Gretchen is on his left. Foxy is at the other end of the table with Hilary and Rose on either side of her. They all turn their attention to the food. It feels good to be eating under the warm sun. At one point, Gretchen turns to Pete. "I knew your mother," she says matter-of-factly.

"It wouldn't surprise me," Pete says, raising his coffee cup as if in a toast. "It wouldn't surprise me at all." Gretchen smiles.

Sometimes, actually a lot of the times, the things Gretchen says are complete *non sequiturs*. Pete suspects, however, that, although they seem distinctly unrelated to anything in the real world, they are related to the world of Gretchen's delusions, and, in that world, they are relevant, even coherent. Pete told Foxy that talking with Gretchen was a little like talking to someone in a dream state. The symbols and metaphors that she uses are unique to her, but that doesn't mean they don't make sense, if only to her. They make an internal sense. What was interesting, Pete said, was when Gretchen extrapolates something from her own non-ordinary reality that provides insight into the ordinary reality where, as he says, "the rest of us live."

Foxy refers to Pete's theories as the "Don Juan school of amateur psychiatry." Her own views are more orthodox, formed, as they were within the halls of orthodox medicine; even though she no longer lives there. After becoming increasingly tired of stringing together low paying, generally un-stimulating jobs as a waitress or clerical worker of some kind, Foxy used her knowledge and her academic credits to get herself certified as a clinical social worker in Massachusetts. Her desire to help people carried her that far back toward her original goal—back in her other life—of becoming a psychiatrist. She is very overqualified for her current position, but that is as far as she can go. Her original goal was too inextricably linked to Desmond, the part of her that was killed; the part of her that stays fixed in time, that doesn't age, that doesn't mature. That never lets go.

~ ~ ~

After lunch, Pete gets passes for everyone—they are in the shape of little animals—and, after everyone gets over admiring their passes, he hands out trail maps.

"There's no cell service here. I think we should try to stick together," Pete says, standing at the end of the picnic table. "Everyone chose a buddy." He looks down at Foxy, who already has Hilary on one arm and Rose on the other. Foxy smiles and shrugs.

Watching Hilary and Rose hook on to Foxy, Gretchen puts her arm through Pete's. Pete, in turn, loops his arm around Willie's, and the three of them lead the way to the entrance of the park. Bud and Slate come next, followed by Marge and Anna. Foxy, Hilary, and Rose follow behind.

The Dead Woman in His Room

Within the first hundred yards, they are hopelessly separated, but it's such a nice day and such a pleasant place to be that it doesn't seem to matter. They can see each other across a distance as the trails meander between the different fenced-in areas. Hilary and Rose take Foxy with them to the man-made rock mountain where the mountain goats and sheep sun themselves. Slate wants to see the buffalo family and, taking Bud's left hand, he directs a course toward the outside pasture. Marge and Anna follow them.

Not being enough of a disciplinarian to coral them together, Pete tries to position himself where he can see everyone at the same time and manages, in the process, to fall behind Gretchen and Willie who are both good walkers and have proceeded ahead on a trail that extends up a slight hill into the woods. Neither of them seems particularly interested in the animals, and they walk along the trail without stopping. Everyone else is stopping. The sun is shining. It's a very tranquil scene. The animals are obviously enjoying the sun, too. There are no natural predators here.

~~~

Nick stays out of the park. He came as close as the parking lot and watched the procession as Pete and his companions made their way to the picnic area. He knows an unaccompanied middle-aged male would stand out suspiciously in this crowd. Instead, he stays out of sight in his U-Rent van and waits. Nick always trails his targets before a hit. He's proven to himself many times that knowing the patterns and habits of his targets makes the risk that he might be seen worth taking. He's very good at stalking his prey.

Usually, it means waiting outside of nightclubs or hotels and office buildings. Nick knows how to be invisible in back streets and warehouse districts. He would have been able to blackmail most of the people he killed if he hadn't killed them. But he doesn't know how to blend in at a petting zoo. This whole scene is weird. He's not comfortable around old people and kids, and he is very uncomfortable around crazy people. He has a sense that they can feel his presence when no one else can. He can feel them, and he doesn't like the way it feels at all. Seeing all the families with kids wandering around the fields with sheep and goats and a bunch of barnyard animals is like watching a parade of the weak. It makes him think about things he doesn't want to think about. It makes him angry. He wishes he had a cigarette, even though he quit years ago. He decides to drive around the other side of the property and see if there isn't a way to come up through the woods where he would be less obvious.

~~~

"Do I know you?" Willie asks abruptly, stopping on the trail and turning to Gretchen. "Are we together?"

"Compared to what?" Gretchen says. The two of them stand facing each other on the trail. Their brains are processing like crazy, but they aren't coming up with anything else to say.

Pete runs back to the edge of the woods to see if he can see where everyone else is. He can't. He looks back and sees Willie and Gretchen standing in the middle of the trail and decides it's safe to leave them long enough to make a quick dash to the brow of the hill where he thinks he'll be able to look out over the whole park. He isn't particularly worried, at this point, but he does take his responsibility for this group very personally.

Pete is very new at this sort of thing. His experience as a parent was so brief, and so many years ago that he never matured into the role. He wants to be in control so that nothing bad happens to the people in his charge, and he hasn't had time to learn that the fundamental experience of being a parent is realizing over and over again that you are not in control. He was certainly not in control when he got arrested for drunkenness when his daughter was three years old. He couldn't remember getting drunk. He couldn't remember the fight. He could remember the last time he saw his daughter. He was sitting in a car on Mulberry Street in the Mission District in San Francisco, and he watched his wife load the last few things into a rented truck the day she left for Phoenix. He sat in the car and watched his wife carry their daughter to the truck and drive away. He promised her he would stay away; and he did. That was the end of his parenting.

Pete sobered up about three years later. The first time. That had lasted almost seven years. He realizes it has been just over seven years since the last time he had a drink. Staying sober and staying away have become linked in his mind. They are the two hardest things he has ever done, and one seems to buttress the other. He can stay sober when he stays away. It has become who he is; except now he isn't sure he could leave, much less stay away.

Pete looks down from the hill across the fields of the animal farm. It's pretty here, and it's warm for late September in the Berkshires. He can see a few trees whose leaves have already started to change colors. He likes being able to look across the broad valley to the range of rounded peaks on the western horizon. He didn't realize the trail they followed into the edge of the woods was so steep.

Looking down across the expanse of the petting zoo fields, the first person he sees is Bud. The white cane catches his eye. Bud is standing next to Anna. Then he sees Marge and Slate standing with their fingers hooked on the fence around a field with a small herd of spotted antelope.

He looks for Foxy and remembers her telling him how she got her nickname. It was back in County Donegal when she was a little girl and lived on a farm. She used to run through the fields below their house. One day her father commented to her when she joined him on the porch that all he could see of her in the tall grass was her bright red hair. "You look like a little red fox out there," he said. "I think we should have called you Foxy." She liked that. The nickname was about all she took with her when her scores on a national exam earned her a full scholarship at a school for gifted children in London. She was 12 when she went away to school. She never really went home after that.

Foxy's red hair has a grey streak through it now. Pete sees her standing with Hilary by the row of portable toilets over near a storage shed. He has to laugh. The thing he likes most about Hilary and Rose is that they were generally and genuinely interested in just about everything, although things having to do with going to the bathroom do seem to hold a special fascination.

He watches the people on the trails for a while, ambling along, the parents talking to each other, the children staring at the animals and the animals looking back at them, disinterestedly. He feels a fondness for this place. It's a gentle place. Having located all the members of his group, he lingers on the brow of the hill watching the scene below.

~~~

While he's gone, Willie tells Gretchen about Nick Barons. "I keep seeing this person, but I can't remember who he is. Does that happen to you?"

"Most of the time," Gretchen says without hesitation. "Is he a real person, or the other kind?"

"I think he's real. I think he's Nick Barons. I remember the name, but I can't remember the person."

"I don't like Nick," Gretchen says.

"Do you know Nick?" Willie sounds surprised.

"Nick, Nick, Nick. I don't like Nick." Each time she says the name she emphasized the k-sound on the end.

"I've seen him. Have you seen him, too?"

"Who?"

"Nick."

"Nick, Nick, Nick."

"Nick Barons."

"Nick, Nick, Nick."

"Stop that. Stop saying that." Willie looks around. He's becoming agitated. "I think I've seen Nick Barons, and I think he's not a good person. But I can't remember how I know that. I can't remember." He stamps his feet. "Where *are* we?"

"I'm going away," Gretchen says. "I won't go with them."

"Go where? What are you talking about?"

"Where lost is."

"What?"

"Not again. Nick, Nick, Nick. No, no, no."

"What are you saying?" Willie looks hard at Gretchen. "Who are you? I don't remember you." Willie looks around. When he looks back, Gretchen is gone.

Gretchen is surprisingly fast for her age. All her walking and nervous energy keeps her in good shape. She takes the trail deeper into the woods. The sign says: "To Llama Lookout – 1/4 mi." She goes that way.

11

"How long has she been gone?"

Willie is standing in the middle of the trail when Pete returns from his reconnaissance. He seems stiff.

"Willie?" Pete says. "Are you okay? Has something happened?" Pete thinks his uncle may have had a stroke. He doesn't really know what happens when a person has a stroke, but the way his uncle looks makes him think that something has let go in his brain.

"Willie!" he tries to snap him out of it. "Willie." He looks into his eyes. "Willie. Please. Willie. Answer me. Willie!"

Willie smiles as if he'd just been turned back on. "Pete. What are you yelling for? I'm right here."

Pete stands up very straight and takes a deep breath. "I thought you checked out there for a minute, Willie."

"What do you mean?"

"Nothing, Willie. Just an expression…hey, Where's Gretchen?" He looks around the immediate area. "Willie, where is Gretchen?"

"Who?"

"Oh. Jesus." He starts looking in a broader area. "Did you see which way she went, Willie?"

"Who?"

"Gretchen, Willie. Did you see which way Gretchen went?"

Willie seems to seriously consider this question for a moment. Then he says, "No."

Pete looks both ways down the trail. He doesn't see anybody in either direction. He looks into the woods. He looks down at the trail itself. He can see where Willie and Gretchen stood talking to each other, shuffling their feet in the gravel. She obviously didn't go down the trail or she would have run into him. It doesn't look as if she went off the trail into the woods. Pete looks the other way on the trail and sees the sign: "Llama Lookout – 1/4mi." The first thing that comes to mind is that Llama Lookout would be a cliff.

"Oh. Jesus." He takes Willie by both arms and looks directly in his eyes. "Willie. Can I trust you to wait right here, and not go anywhere? I have to go find Gretchen. Will you wait for me here, Willie?"

Willie's eyes don't say yes.

There's a bench about 20 yards down the trail toward the main compound. Pete escorts Willie to the bench and sits him down on it. "I want you to sit here, Willie, until I get back. I'm only going to be gone a short time. Can you wait here for me, Willie?"

Willie looks up at Pete from the bench. "I want you to stay here until I come back, Willie. Okay? Don't go anywhere until I come back. Understood." Willie seems to shake his head.

Pete sprints down the trail toward the top of the hill where he went to look for everyone before. That already seems like hours ago. He stops once to look back and see Willie sitting where he left him, and then races down the hill.

They are all there, less than 100 yards away, standing together around a fence where an emu and a fawn have come over to see if they have any food. He feels such huge relief when he sees them all, it feels like love. They are there.

Foxy is the first to see him coming and she takes a few steps away from the group to approach him. He almost runs into her.

"Gretchen is gone. I left her and Willie for a few moments to see where you all were and when I got back, Gretchen was gone. Willie has no idea where she went or why. I left him on a bench beside the trail. We have to go back. Somebody has to stay with him while I find Gretchen." It all came out in rush. "God. I'm glad I found you." He almost kisses her.

Foxy looks at him for a moment and then turns to Marge. "Marge, Gretchen is missing. Get everybody together and bring them up this trail. I'll be waiting up there with Willie. Pete is going to go look for Gretchen. Please hurry." Then she turns back toward Pete. "Let's go," she says and sprints back the way Pete came. He has to dig in to catch up with her.

"How long has she been gone?" Foxy asks without slowing down.

"Not long. Minutes. She and Willie were talking, and I just went back to look for you guys. Just to see where you all were. Minutes. No more than that." They are both running hard now.

"Do you know why she left?"

"No."

"How's Willie?"

"He's out of it. I thought he had stroke."

"He might have," Foxy says. They run on in silence until they approach Willie on the bench. "Which way are you going to go?" Foxy asks Pete.

"Toward the Lookout," Pete points toward the sign.

Foxy raises her eyebrows. "Okay. I'll follow as soon as they get here. Listen for me. I have a whistle." Pete looks at her. "Go!" she says. "Go! Willie will be all right."

Pete runs on. He takes the fork in the trail toward Llama Lookout, running slower now so he can scan the woods on both sides of the trail. The woods are fairly open, and he can see a considerable distance. Gretchen is nowhere to be seen. As the trail climbs, the woods get thicker. Running feels good. The air is cool in the woods, and the gravel trail provides good traction. He can see an opening where the trail passes over the crest of a hill. Beyond that would be the Lookout. His mind races ahead. Would there be a cliff at the Lookout? Would Gretchen jump? She was schizophrenic, but that didn't mean she was suicidal. Why had she run away? Had she run away or was she just wandering aimlessly? What if she wasn't at the Lookout? What if she was…?

He pulls a trail map out of his back pocket and scans it as he runs. The trail to Llama Lookout is a loop off the main trail which extends into a large area marked "Safari Land." From there, as near as he can tell looking at the map while he runs, the trail joins a dirt road that leads back to the main compound. If she stays on the trail, she'll wind up right back at the beginning; he tells himself. He is approaching the crest of the hill and realizes the land drops off abruptly beyond the crest. He runs harder.

Gretchen isn't at the Lookout. At least she isn't on his side of the stonewall that forms an arc where the trail widens below him. From where he is, he can see across a broad valley, but he can't tell how abruptly the land breaks on the other side of the wall. He can't tell if it's a cliff or just a steep slope. As much as he wants to see Gretchen, he doesn't want to see her on the other side of that wall. He sprints to the wall. The wall is three feet wide and almost four feet tall. It was clearly meant to keep people away from the edge of the cliff on the other side that drops a good 40 feet into the woods below. Pete scrambles over the wall and eases out on to the edge of the cliff. He leans out as far as he can, but he can't see the bottom of the cliff.

"Damn." He'll have to work his way down around the side of the cliff to make sure Gretchen isn't lying at the bottom. The fact of the cliff somehow makes the prospect of her lying at the bottom more plausible. He scrambles back on top of the stone wall and follows it as fast as he can to the end that extends into the slope just beyond the cliff. He jumps off the wall on to the steep slope, and, grabbing saplings and skidding on the loose rocks and leaves, he works his way down toward the face of the cliff, stopping a few times to lean out and look for the bottom. He hates how much time this is taking. What if she is there? What if she isn't there? Behind those immediate questions is the darker thought that Gretchen has gotten lost on his watch. If he hadn't left her alone with Willie, this wouldn't have happened. How could he leave them alone in the woods? A chronic schizophrenic and a senile old man. What was he thinking?

His foot slips out from under him, and he falls back hard against the ground and slides downhill on his butt. It carries him down slope, at least. He can almost see the bottom. It looks like the opening to a cave. "Oh. Jesus." Scratched and sore he arrives panting at the bottom. No cave. No Gretchen. He looks up. He looks down, deeper into the woods. Nothing. He's relieved. But Gretchen is still missing.

Then he hears a whistle. He moves away from the bottom of the cliff and looks up. He can see the top of the cliff, but he can't see anyone. He takes one last look around and then leans into the hill and scrambles back up the route he just came down.

"Pete," he hears. "Pete are you down there? Pete," Then the whistle again.

He can see her now. Foxy has climbed over the stone wall but has kept as far away from the cliff as she can on that side of the wall. He can tell from the way she clings to the stonewall that she doesn't like being there. But she is there, nonetheless. "Pete," she yells.

"Over here. Foxy. I'm here," Pete yells back. "She's not here. I checked. I went to the bottom."

"Okay," she says. "I'll meet you." She climbs back over the wall and is waiting at the end of it when Pete pulls himself up the last of the steep slope. He stands leaning against the stonewall, panting. His shirt is torn, and he has scratches on his arms. Foxy hands him a water bottle that she takes from a fanny pack. He drinks in gulps and hands the bottle back to her.

"Thanks," he says. "At least she's not there. How's Willie?"

"Willie's fine. I think he just got disoriented. I asked Marge to take him back to the van. He loves that van of yours. I think he'll feel safer there. It's familiar. She's going to stay with him. And

Bud said he would, too. Marge gave me this," Foxy pulled a bright yellow walkie-talkie from her pack. "Anna's got the other one."

Pete turns the walkie-talkie over in his hand and laughs. "10-4 good buddy,"

Foxy looks at him uncomprehendingly.

"It's part of the lingo. You know, CB radios, walkie-talkies. Over and out."

"America."

"Yeah," he says. "You read me." They smile at each other.

"Let's try it out." He holds the yellow handset up to his mouth. "Marge," he says. "Marge. Anna. Are you there?" He looks at Foxy, "I don't know what the range is on these things."

Pete holds the handset away from him when Anna's voice booms out. "Anna here. Do you read me? Pete, is that you?"

He can't help laughing. "Pete here. 10-4 good buddy," he smiles at Foxy. "I read you loud and clear. What's your 20?"

"What?" Anna says. They hear Marge's voice in the background, "Where are you? Tell him where you are. That's your 20."

"Oh." Anna says. "We're at the van. In the parking lot." They hear Marge's voice again in the background, "What's your 20? Now you ask him: what's your 20?" And then Anna's voice, a little louder, "What's your 20?"

"Llama Lookout." Pete says, stifling a laugh. "Gretchen is not here."

"Oh."

"Foxy and I are going to follow the trail from here that leads back through the woods toward you. Hopefully, we'll find Gretchen somewhere along the trail. We'll call if we see her. You do the same, okay?"

"What?"

"Call us if you see Gretchen. She might come there."

"Oh."

"Okay. 10-4. Talk to you later," Pete says.

"10-4," Anna says. "Over and out."

Pete hands the walkie-talkie to Foxy and takes his trail map out of his back pocket. "We're here," he says pointing to the map. "The trail loops around through Safari Land and heads back toward the compound where the barns are. I'm thinking we ought to follow that and see if we see her. Hopefully, she'll stay on the trail."

"We'll find her, Pete." Foxy says, looking up from the map. "Gretchen walks around Mill River all the time, and she always finds her way back. Are there any cross trails that lead away?"

"God, I hope not." He takes a deep breath. "You ready?"

Foxy nods, and they take off running at a fast jog.

~~~

Willie seems very content to clamber up into his seat in Pete's van and wait for the others. Bud sits in the driver's seat. All the doors are open, and it makes the van feel like a big tent. Marge and Anna dig into the food baskets and put together a round of seconds from lunch for everyone. Slate sits on the bench seat in the back of the van, leaning up against the side where he is right behind Bud. Hilary and Rose seem to be getting a kick out of being able to climb in and out of the van and are trying out all the seats, recalling where everyone sat on the way here.

"I'm Marge." "I'm Anna." "I'm Bud." They say as they move around inside the van, sitting for a moment in each place. "I'm Rose," Hilary says sitting in Rose's seat. "I'm Hilary," Rose says, shoving in beside her. They clearly think they are on to something wonderful, and the van rocks as they change places. They are less pleased with the indifferent reaction from their captive audience. Bud, Willie, and Slate ignore them. Marge and Anna are at the back door, putting the food away. Occasionally, Hilary and Rose peek over the backseat at the two of them. "Hi Marge. Hi Anna. Peek-a-boo."

"We're going to have to do something with these two," Marge says to Anna as they get the food containers tucked away. "I think they're getting a little wound up. Either that or I'm getting a little wound down."

"Maybe we could take them somewhere close," Anna offers. "There's a big blue barn just past the gift shop where I think they have baby animals. Maybe we could take them there. It's not far."

Marge considers the idea and settles on a plan. "Anna, you stay here at the van with Bud and Willie. I'll take Hilary and Rose to the barn. Keep the walkie talkie with you and make sure it's on. If you hear anything, you can send Slate to find us. Okay?"

Anna looks a little apprehensively at the walkie-talkie.

"You'll be fine. Just press the button when you want to talk. If you have a problem, Bud can help you." Anna isn't entirely convinced, but she agrees.

Hilary and Rose are very excited to be going to see the baby animals. When Marge tells them they have to be on their best behavior and stay together, Hilary grabs Rose's hand with her left hand and grabs Marge's hand with her right. She beams. Rose, however, shakes off her sister's hand and comes around to the other side of Marge and grabs her right hand. Hilary looks over at her unhappily.

"This could get interesting," Marge says, setting off for the barn. "I think we're getting tired."

Anna climbs into the van and sits next to Slate on the seat behind Bud and Willie. She explains the plan to Bud and says she'll stay in the van with them if they don't mind. She seems a little nervous about being left behind with the men. It isn't her usual place.

"Welcome aboard," Bud says. Willie doesn't say anything. He's been pre-occupied with his thoughts since returning to the van.

Bud turns back toward Anna. "That was great lunch, by the way," he says to her, adding, "I was a cook you know?"

"Really? I didn't know."

"Yeah, in the navy, and then in the merchant marine. I cooked onboard ship all over the world."

"I love to cook, too," Anna says. "We'll have to exchange recipes," she flushes when she realizes what she said. "Oh. I'm sorry."

"Hey. It's all in here," Bud taps his head. "I have all the recipes in my head where I can see 'em. I don't cook that much anymore," he adds. "Most of my recipes were for 20 or 30 sailors, anyway."

"Maybe I can cook dinner for you some time," Anna says. "You and Willie and Slate," she adds quickly, looking around sheepishly.

"I'd like that Anna," Bud says. "I'm sure Willie would, too. How about you Slate? Slate?"

Slate is looking out the window at Marge and Hilary and Rose. He kind of wants to go to the baby animal barn with them, but he doesn't want to say anything. He's never been to a place like this.

Reading Slate's silence, Bud says, "Hey, Slate. Maybe you should go over there with them. Just so you know where they are. Then you could come back here in case we need you for anything. Sound like a plan?"

"Yeah," Slate says. "Yeah, okay if you want. Then I'll know the way. I'll come right back."

"Don't rush. I'm sure we'll be fine," Bud says. "Anna can always go over if we hear anything on the walkie-talkie. Is that okay with you, Anna?"

"Yes. That's fine," Anna says. Slate is already out the door.

The baby animal barn is more than a hundred yards away from where the van is in the parking lot. Slate catches up to the others about halfway there. Marge looks back toward the van and waves acknowledgement, tugging Rose's arm into the air to accomplish it.

~~~

Pete and Foxy stop running and settle into a fast walk. They are both in good shape, but they are not young. Pete also worked hard getting down to the bottom of the cliff and back up to the trail, and he feels the strain in his knees. By now it's midafternoon, and the sun is slanting through the woods. They become more aware of each other, walking fast, and breathing hard.

"Do you think she'd stay on the trail?" Pete asks.

"I think so," Foxy says. "But it's hard to know. I didn't think she'd ever get in the van in the first place. She must like you."

"I guess," Pete says, shaking his head. "Maybe I shouldn't have brought her along. I feel like I've put her at huge risk."

"Life is risky, Pete. I think bringing her along was an act of generosity. Gretchen hasn't seen much generosity. She's been treated as if she didn't exist most of her life. A little compassion is worth the risk. I bet we'll find her somewhere safe."

"I hope so."

They are coming to where the hiking trail they are on meets the dirt road through Safari Land. They are going to have to split up to cover the full loop around Safari Land.

"I'll take the high road, if you'll take the low road," Pete says.

Foxy reaches into her fanny pack. "You better take the walkie-talkie. I don't know how to use this thing, anyway. I've got my whistle. I'll blow it three times if I find Gretchen."

"Okay. But I don't have a whistle. How will I communicate with you?"

"I'll just follow the trail all the way back. We'll meet back at the van. Who knows. Gretchen might already be there."

"You'll be all right?" Pete asks her.

Foxy laughs. "I'll be fine. I'll probably beat you, so you better get started."

They look at each other, briefly, and then set off jogging in different directions.

12

"Not your fault, man. Not your fault."

The atmosphere in the blue barn is muted. Most of the light comes in from two huge double doors that face south. As you move inside it gets darker. The main room is long enough for perspective to make the corridor that runs down the middle appear to narrow toward the far end. Light comes in from windows on the far wall. On both sides, all along the corridor, are pens with animals too young to be let out on their own in the fields. Loose hay and dust soften all the angles, and the smell of warm manure makes the air feel close. Sounds seem to rise vertically and disappear into the rafters overhead, isolating each pen in its own acoustic environment of squealing and bleating baby goats and lambs. A teenage girl just inside the front doors sells little paper cups full of feed for people to give to the baby animals.

    Like barkers on a midway, the baby animals know how to spot a soft touch, and they spot Hilary and Rose immediately, straining their little necks through the rails on the side of the pens, and pushing each other out of the way to get to them first. After one of the larger goats takes the whole cup, feed and all from Hilary's hand, Marge shows Hilary and Rose how to pour a small amount of feed in the palm of their hands and then let the little animals lick a few pieces at a time. They squeal with laughter each time a little goat or lamb tickles their hands with their nibbling lips. Very few women as old Hilary and Rose are capable of such unabashed joy as the two forty-something sisters demonstrate in that barn that afternoon. There aren't any other people in the barn at this point. The fall sun is already getting low in the sky and people are starting to go home.

Standing far enough inside the barn to begin to make out the scene ahead of him, Slate is appalled. He didn't know what to expect when he entered the feeding barn, but he has seen something like this frantic, straining, pushing, grabbing, licking, sucking behavior before, and seeing it in the faces of all these little animals is like walking into a nightmare. Marge didn't notice him drop behind as she followed Hilary and Rose deeper into the barn. In the shadows, made deeper by his dark glasses, Slate sees images of his mother and her latest boyfriend Wayne. He has seen them pulling and grabbing and licking and sucking with the same frenzy he sees in the faces of the little animals. He has seen that same stupid-eyed pleading-yet-resolute look in Wayne's face coming for him in his bed. He thought it only happened there. In his house.

Slate is backing up when he bumps into a tall elderly man in overalls who entered the barn after him. Feeling the man's legs behind him, Slate spins around so abruptly that his sunglasses fall from his face. He starts to grab for them, but he sees the tall man looming over him and runs for the door. The light seems doubly bright when he gets outside, and he stumbles and falls, scraping the palm of his left hand when he hits the ground. He's crying now, and, in his blurred vision, he can't tell if anyone is chasing him. No one is.

Slate runs around a parked tractor and works his way along the outside of the barn, stopping on the far side of a rain barrel where he knows he'll be out of sight. He leans against the barn and picks at the dirt that is jammed into the scrapes on the palm of his hand. He's on the east side of the barn, and it's starting to get cold. He sits down and hugs his knees in front of him and cries quietly. He didn't expect to see that look here, away from home, with his new friends.

The tall man in overalls is Bill Riley, the owner, operator and chief cook and bottle washer of the Sky Meadow Wildlife Farm. When he couldn't survive financially as a dairy farmer on the land that his great grandfather had first cleared, he came up with the idea of the wildlife petting zoo and, with the help of his two granddaughters, he managed to get a federal grant that was almost big enough to support it. Riley compensates for the shortfall of funds with his genuine love of all animals, which extends to most of the visitors. Tall and grey-haired with a wrinkled face and bright blue eyes, Riley and his granddaughters have managed to care for the animals and keep the gates open for the last ten years.

~~~

Anna pours Bud another cup of coffee to go with a slice of her minced pie. The van is in a section of the parking area that is still sunny, and warm. Bud and Anna are talking about cooking. Anna never cooked for any group larger than an extended family, and she's fascinated by Bud's stories about how he managed an onboard kitchen that could serve 30 men for extended periods of time at sea.

During a pause in their conversation, Bud wonders why Slate hasn't returned to the van yet. Even given the distractions Bud anticipates Slate might have encountered in the barn, he thought he'd be back by now. "I wonder what's keeping Slate?" he thinks out loud. "Seems like he's been gone a long time."

"I could go look for him, if you want," Anna volunteers. "I don't mind. I'm sure he's in the barn with Marge and the girls." Anna finds herself wanting to do things for Bud and she enjoys the feeling. "Now you've got me wondering. I'll go right now, and I'll come right back. Do you want another piece of pie before I go?"

"Thank you, no. I'm stuffed. I should be outside doing jumping jacks. Maybe Willie and I will do some jumping jacks while you're gone. What do you say, Willie?"

Willie seems to be listening to music in his head. He's nodding rhythmically.

"Oh well." Bud says. "I guess we won't do any jumping jacks."

"I'll be right back," Anna says, sliding the back door of the van closed. She looks for a moment through the side-door window at Bud in the driver's seat before she sets off for the barn. She has her purse with the walkie-talkie inside.

Marge is talking to Bill Riley when Anna gets to the barn with the news that Slate has not returned to the van.

"He was here," Marge says. "But after I got Hilary and Rose started, I turned around and he was gone. I just assumed he'd gone back to the van."

"Excuse me for overhearing, but a kid about seven or eight bumped into me a little while ago," Riley says. "He ran out of here like he'd seen a ghost. I didn't know who he was with at the time. Kids sometimes have strange reactions to the feeding barn. We get a lot of city kids here."

"That must have been Slate," Marge says. "Maybe he had to go to the bathroom or something."

"Listen, if you want to go look for him, go ahead," Riley says. "I've got some work to do in the barn, and I don't mind keeping an eye on your friends. One of my daughters had Down's Syndrome. She loved this barn. They remind me a little of her."

Marge considers his offer and decides he can be trusted. "Thank you. We'll come back as soon as we find Slate. And if we don't find him right away," Marge adds, "I'll come back for Hilary and Rose."

"They'll be fine," Riley says.

"He seems very nice," Anna says as they emerge from the barn into the afternoon sunlight.

"Yes." Marge seems distracted by the comment. "Why would he run out of the barn like that? I don't understand."

"Maybe he had to go to the bathroom."

"Good idea. I'll go down to the port-o-potties. You look in the gift shop and meet me back here."

"Marge! Anna!" It's Foxy. She just completed her loop of the outer trail system. "Did Gretchen come back?" she asks as she jogs up to them. Her face is flushed, and strands of her red hair are plastered to her neck with sweat. "Is Pete here?"

"No." Marge says. "Pete's not here. Gretchen didn't come back, and now we can't find Slate, either."

"What?" Foxy is stretching her back from side to side, and she jerks upright. "When did this happen?" She's still breathing a little heavy from her jog.

"We just found out. He came to the barn with me and Hilary and Rose and, at some point, he ran out. We don't know why he ran out, but he didn't go back to the van."

"We better call Pete," Foxy says. "He went the long way around the trail, but he should be here soon. I guess he didn't find Gretchen, or he would have called."

Marge and Foxy look at Anna. "What?" Anna says.

"The walkie-talkie, Anna. Do you have your walkie-talkie?"

"Yes." Anna says, sounding pleasantly surprised as she looks up from her purse. "Yes, I do," she repeats. She gives the walkie-talkie to Marge.

"Pete? Pete? Do you read me? It's Marge. Come in Pete." She lets her thumb off the speech button and holds the yellow handset in front of her after she speaks so they can all hear.

"Pete. Pete. Come in. It's Marge," She repeats.

"Hey Marge," Pete's voice comes through. "Is Gretchen with you?"

"No, Pete, Gretchen is not here."

"Damn. I hoped she would be. Is Foxy there?"

"Yes, Foxy is here, but, Pete, now Slate is missing."

"What!?"

"He came to the feeding barn with us, and Riley saw him run out…"

"Who's Riley?"

"He's the man who operates the petting zoo."

There's a pause. "Listen, Marge. There's too much going on. Where are you now?"

"We're in front of the feeding barn, the big blue barn."

"Okay, I can see the barn from where I am. I'm just on the hill above the farm. Stay right there until I get there. We've got to work together on this."

"Will do. 10-4," Marge says.

"Yes" Pete says.

Foxy jogs over to where she can see Pete taking long strides as he runs down toward the barn. She watches him approach for a while and then jogs out to meet him.

"Foxy," Pete says. "What's going on? What's this about Slate?"

"I just found out myself, Pete. I just got here."

Pete is winded. He slows to a trot. "I'm sorry. I'm not angry with you. I…"

"I know. Don't worry about me. Marge and Anna are at the barn with Hilary and Rose. It's over this way." They jog together to the barn. Pete is soaked in sweat and his face is very red.

"You okay?" Foxy asks.

"Yeah. I'm okay. Just worried."

They stop when they hit the relative darkness inside the barn. As their eyes adjust, at about the same time, they both realize there's no one there. They look at each other and walk further into the barn.

"Marge," Pete calls. "Marge. Are you in here?" Then louder, "Marge."

They hear a stall gate open several pens deeper into the barn and Marge appears. She waves them over and holds her index finger up in front of her mouth. "Shhhh," she says and points into the stall.

In the center of the stall is a llama lying down, looking like a giant furry bath toy. It's chewing its cud and seems very contented. Next to it, asleep in the straw, are Hilary and Rose.

"I found them here like this," Riley says from the corner of the stall. "It's perfectly safe. Llamas love people."

"Looks like they love llamas, too." Pete says, stepping across the stall and extending his hand, "you must be Riley."

"Yup."

"I guess you've heard about our excitement?"

"Yes. We've had some people missing for a while, but we've never lost anyone here."

"Well," Pete says, "Gretchen is special."

Riley indicates Hilary and Rose.

"Not like that." Pete says. "Gretchen is in her 70s. She spent most of her life in a mental hospital."

"All God's children," Riley says.

"Need traveling shoes," says Pete, hoping to deflect what he guessed was some knee-jerk Biblical reference from Riley.

"Maya Angelou," Riley says to Pete's surprise. "One of my favorites. I used to read *All God's Children Need Traveling Shoes* to my granddaughters."

Pete seems to visibly relax. He takes a deep breath. "Can they stay here with you while we take one more look for Gretchen. If we don't find her soon, I think we'll need to organize a search party."

"I agree." Riley says. "It's going to start getting dark soon. And then it's going to get cold."

Pete steps back out of the stall and Foxy, Marge and Anna come with him.

Turning to Foxy he says, "Why don't you make a loop through the lower fields from the north, and I'll swing around from the south. We'll meet back here."

Then he turns to Marge. "Marge, why don't you stay here with Anna in case Hilary and Rose wake up, or Slate comes back. Call me on the walkie-talkie if he does." They are walking together toward the front of the barn. "I'll meet you back here in ten minutes. No. Make it 15. I want to swing by the van and check on Willie and make sure he's okay." He looks at his watch. "It's 4 o'clock. I'll meet you back here at 4:15." They all nod, and Foxy and Pete take off jogging in different directions.

~~~

Willie isn't aware of how much time has passed when he looks out the side window and sees Gretchen standing there looking at him. He rolls down the window and looks back at her.

"I saw Nick," she says. Willie nods. They look at each other as if in agreement.

Pete runs up just then. "Gretchen," he says and gives her a big hug. "Am I glad to see you. We looked all over for you. Where have you been?"

"I've been right here."

"She saw Nick," Willie says matter-of-factly.

Pete laughs. "I'm going to have to meet this guy, one of these days. Gretchen, why don't you get inside the van and have a seat. I'm going to call Marge and Anna and let them know we've found you." Pete remembers to leave the door open for Gretchen and then comes around to the driver's side door.

"Bud, can I talk to you for a minute outside the van?"

Bud grabs his cane and swings his legs out of the van. "What's up?" He slides to the ground next to Pete.

"It's Slate. Now he's missing."

"Damn."

"Exactly. Do you have any idea why he might want to run off? Did he say anything to you?"

"No. I sent him to the barn with Marge, and when he didn't come back right away Anna went to look for him."

"Well. Anna and Marge are at the barn, but Slate's gone. The guy who runs the place was there and he says he saw a boy about Slate's age run out of the barn like he'd seen a ghost. Now we've found Gretchen, but we've lost Slate."

"Let me go," Bud says, tapping the ground with his cane. "Take me to the barn."

Pete looks at Bud. "Okay with me. Something tells me if anyone can find him, you can. Let me just call Marge and Anna and let them know that Gretchen is here. I'll have Anna come back and stay with Willie and Gretchen while we go to the barn. I'm not leaving those two alone again. That's for sure."

"Not your fault, man," Bud says. "Not your fault."

"Yeah, I guess," Pete says.

~~~

After Anna arrives at the van and settles in the back with Gretchen, Pete and Bud set off for the barn. They've walked together around the grounds of the High Rise so often they automatically fall into position with Pete a little ahead and to the left of Bud. Bud holds his cane in his right hand and taps the trail in front of him. They walk quickly back toward the barn.

Foxy is just arriving in front of the barn when they get there. "I made it all the way around the lower fields, and I didn't see anybody." She says walking over to them.

"Gretchen's at the van," Pete says. "She just showed up on her own. Anna and Willie are with her now. Bud wants to come and help us look for Slate."

"You two go in the barn and let me stand here for a while," Bud says. "My guess is he isn't running away. I think he's hiding. That's what he does."

Standing deep enough inside the barn to be covered in darkness from the outside, Pete and Foxy are joined in the shadows by Marge. From their vantage point they can see across the open area in front of the feeding barn. Bud stands in the middle of the barnyard, turning his head every now and then to unseen sounds. Shadows are creeping into the petting zoo as the late September afternoon sun ducks for the horizon and the breath of the place rises in thin vapors from its warmth. Moist air is teased by the chill into a halo above a trailer with a load of hay that soaked up sun all afternoon. As the light of the sun slants through the earth's atmosphere it filters out colors from the landscape, preparing it for darkness. Shadows cut across the barnyard. Bud stands unmoving. Even his cane is still.

Pete becomes aware that he is holding Foxy's hand. He isn't aware of taking it. Maybe she took his. He isn't sure. He is both physically and emotionally exhausted from rushing somewhere all day. Watching Bud standing in the barnyard is like repeating a mantra that quiets his thoughts and causes him to breathe slower. Time passes.

"What's he doing?" Marge asks softly.

"I don't know exactly," Pete says. "But if anyone can find Slate, it's Bud."

"But he's not looking," Marge says.

"He's waiting," Pete says. "I think what he's doing is waiting."

"But what's he waiting for?" Marge asks.

"He knows he can't look for Slate, so he's letting Slate find him."

Pete and Foxy look at each other and then at Marge. They fall silent again.

At some point, Slate enters the scene, walks quietly up to Bud and takes his left hand. Bud nods and taps his cane twice and they set off together toward the parking area. That was it. If anything is said between them, it isn't heard in the barn.

"I wonder if these could belong to your young man," Riley says, coming up behind where they are standing. He has a pair of sunglasses in his hand. "I found these on floor, but I didn't think they could belong to a boy. Now I see they could." Riley nods his head toward Slate and Bud leaving the barnyard.

"I've got something else here, too," he adds, and steps aside for Hilary and Rose who come up from behind him stretching and yawning.

"We been sleeping," Hilary says, adding proudly, "with a llama."

"Did we miss anything?" Rose asks.

~~~

Pete asks Foxy if she wants to start out driving on the ride back. It's an easy gift to give. She still has the keys. They are the last vehicle to leave the parking lot. Riley walks them to the van and closes the gate behind them when they leave. They drive down the mountains toward Mill River. It's soon dark.

It's quiet in the van. The darkness isolates everyone in his or her own thoughts. The experiences of the day have been bonding. They feel close and comfortable with each other. Foxy is a good driver and the smooth rhythm of the van on the winding roads is relaxing. From where he is sitting in the last row next to Hilary and Rose, Pete can see Foxy's face illuminated in the rearview mirror whenever a car comes from the other direction on the highway and trawls the van with its lights. There weren't many cars, in either direction. Hilary and Rose have already fallen back asleep. Rose has her head on Pete's shoulder. She smells vaguely of llama. He tries to sit so he won't disturb her, but his own head bobs occasionally as sleep takes him as well. Between times, he has the familiar sensation of detachment from the scene he finds himself in, as if he were observing himself with the others in the back of the van.

Pete lived much of his life in the distance between his surroundings and his own point of view, which was always separate. He is a kind of voyeur in that way. He watches other people live their lives. He even watches himself interacting with them. But he isn't with them. He's the observer. He first became aware of the sensation on school breaks after his parents were killed in the car accident. He always went home on school break, but it was never to his home. It was always a classmate's home. Since then, he has lived all over the country, but nowhere felt like home. He was an outsider even in his own life.

Before coming to Mill River, in fact, the distance between Pete and the world he appeared to live in had been expanding. He wrote books about interesting subjects that he could hardly remember after he wrote them. He had a sense that the umbilical cord that attached the part of him that was the observer to the part of him that was the participant would someday dissolve. And he did not fear that eventuality. He knew he risked becoming irrelevant, but he didn't really care. If anything, his will to stay attached to his surroundings had been weakening.

Maybe that's what happened when he drank. The link to the observer was somehow unplugged. He was a black-out drunk and would have no memory of what he had done while he was drunk; usually not after the first few drinks or even the first day, but during the second day or the third. At some point, he functioned without the observer.

Pete was capable of things when he was drunk that he was not capable of when he was sober. There was an anger and a sense of abandon in him when he was drunk that made him dangerous in a self-destructive sort of way. He picked fights with strangers in bars. He wrecked cars. He got lost on the highway, often waking up in the back of his car in some place he didn't remember. He woke up in a booth in the back of a diner in a small town one time, and he had no idea even what state he was in or how he got there. Waking up there was like stepping through the backside of a mirror, back into real life. He wasn't sure which side was more real. It didn't seem to matter. Drinking made things matter. But only to that part of him that drank. The observer was disinterested in what mattered to Pete when he was drunk.

The observer is interested in what is happening to him since he came to Mill River. Nodding off and on between sleep and consciousness in the back of the van, Pete is aware of feeling as if he were an integral part of this strange group of people in the van with him. Hilary and Rose; Bud and Slate; Marge, Gretchen, and Anna; Willie and Foxy. He feels connected to them somehow. He feels in touch with them. It could have been a dream, but it feels more like waking up.

Foxy is awake. As she maneuvers Pete's van down the mountain road toward Mill River, her mind navigates roads she has not taken in a long time. Foxy cares for people. It's who she is and what she does. What is different now is that she cares for these specific people. A desire to care for people motivated her through medical school, but the first specific person she truly cared for as an adult was Desmond. After he was killed, she still cared for people, but she never loved anyone. And, if anyone had loved her, she wasn't aware of it, nor could she have been. There was no reaching her.

Pete reached her without trying; without either of them trying. They didn't either one of them understand what was going on, only that they now feel different about life and somehow the change seems to emanate from each other. But the changes aren't limited to how they feel about each other. The way they feel about everything is changing. Foxy not only feels drawn to Pete, but she also feels closer to Gretchen and Hilary and Rose and her other patients. They impinge on her professionalism uncomfortably. She is becoming vested in each of them and, in the process, each of them takes a piece of her with them. It's unnerving. She hasn't thought that falling in love would change her relationship to everyone; just to one person.

In the rearview mirror, she sees Pete's head bobbing in the back of the van. Was he aware of this? She knows, but she isn't sure. Her head and her heart are of two minds. She always related to the Little Prince when she read Saint-Exupery's novel. Now, sometimes, she feels like the rose. This was all very different. It summons feelings she hasn't known in a long time. It also summons fears she thought she had conquered but had only avoided.

~~~

Nick follows from a safe distance. He doesn't know what to make of the day he's just had. He knows Willie from the picture he took from the apartment, and he guesses the tall skinny guy is Pete, his nephew. But who the hell were all the other people? The world Nick lives in is violent and amoral, but it also crudely logical. People did things for a reason. And, even if the reasons were concealed, Nick learned that, if he watched people long enough, he could see the reasons. Fear and greed, and their derivatives: power, money, and sex. It was always one of those. He could always tell.

What he saw today was nuts. Nick didn't make his kind of living following people to petting zoos. If this was a cover, it was the most elaborate one he's ever seen. It was unnerving. This morning he felt close to getting back what his father stole from him. Now he feels as if the money and getting even are somehow being taken back. He is losing it all over again. Fucking petting zoo. He feels as if he is being made a fool of. The taillights of Pete's van mock him from a distance. Sometimes he gets much too close, and it takes all his strength to keep from ramming the van. He drops back, but then he focuses on those two red lights again, and he gets closer and closer. He's losing it. The rage is taking over. He has to do something soon.

13

"Get in!"

Nick parks on the side street that runs by the High Rise. As he watches the van park under a streetlight in the High Rise parking lot, he notices movement in his rear view mirror. It's Kenny. He has a crumpled paper sack in his hands. Nick rolls down the window next to the sidewalk.

"Kenny," he calls as Kenny gets even with the van. When Kenny stops and turns, Nick pushes the door open in front of him. "Get in!"

When the dome light in the van shows Nick leaning across the seat toward him, Kenny rocks backwards, but he comes forward. He knows he can't run from somebody like Nick. He climbs unsteadily onto the seat. "Hey, my man," he says. "Where you been?" Then he holds out his paper bag. "You want some?"

Nick jerks the bag out of his hand and tosses it into the back of the van. "You're on duty," he says. "I want to know who those people are." Nick points to the people getting out of Pete's van. Where Nick is parked, they can see the van through the windshield. It's about 20 yards away, down a slight hill.

"Whatever you say." Kenny leans forward in his seat and puts his hands on the dashboard to steady himself. His head seems loose on his neck. He peers through the window.

Foxy is the first one out of the van.

The Dead Woman in His Room

"That one, that one with the red hair, that's Foxy," Kenny says her name with an emphasis on the last syllable that gives it a hissing sound. "I hate that bitch. Miss Goody Two-Shoes. She's got an English accent and thinks she's so smart. She's a shrink, or something, always talking to the crazies in the building; and sticking her nose in other people's business. Rumor is she's screwing your guy Pete." Kenny adds, looking over at Nick. "Not too goodie-goodie for a good fuck, apparently."

"Where does she live?" Nick asks.

"Hey. I don't know," Kenny looks back toward the van. "She won't fuck me. There!" he points. "There's your guy. That old guy with the white hair is Willie. And that other guy, the tall skinny guy," Kenny says, "that's Pete, Willie's nephew. He's the one who lives in that dump on River Street where they found the dead woman a few nights ago." Kenny looks sideways at Nick to see his reaction to this connection. Nick just stares out the window into the parking lot.

"Oh, Christ!" Kenny sneers. "They've been on one of their little field trips."

Marge comes out of the van backwards, her sweat suited butt leading the way. Marge is long past worrying about being dainty. Anna comes out basically the same way, with just a little more femininity. "The first one, with the big ass, that's Marge. Her son's a cop. I went to high school with him. He comes around here every Sunday. The other one is Anna. One of her kids was a doper. He OD'd in his garage after he got kicked out of the Army."

"See the one with the flag around her head. That's our resident schizo. Walks around talking to herself all day." They both sit back when Gretchen turns and looks up toward them.

"She gives me the creeps," Kenny says, looking away.

When Hilary and Rose get out of the van, Kenny scoffs, "Those two! They shouldn't let people like that in this building. They're retards. I don't know their names."

Bud and Slate get out of the van last.

The Dead Woman in His Room

"The blind guy, that's Bud something or other, "Kenny says. "He lives on the other side of Willie. Where I live. On the fifth floor. I don't know who the kid is. I never seen him before."

"You didn't say that you lived down the hall from Willie," Nick says. "Did you forget to mention that?"

"Hey. I didn't get around to it yet."

"What's your apartment number?"

"I'm just down from Willie."

"What's the number Kenny? Don't fuck with me."

"505. Okay," Kenny says. "Willie's in 509. Two doors down."

"Who's in the middle?"

"Middle?"

"Between you and Willie."

"Oh. A guy named Ralph. I don't know anything about him. He and Willie and the blind guy. They take walks around the grounds sometimes. That's all I know."

"You live alone, Kenny?"

"Ah…no."

"Who do you live with?"

"I live with a woman, okay? She got the apartment. She's on disability. I moved in a couple of years ago. I thought you wanted to know about Willie."

"What's her name?"

"Who?"

"Your woman."

"Jen. Her name is Jen, okay."

Nick looks at Kenny for a long time, then, looking back toward the parking lot he adds, "You did good." Nick puts his right hand on the back of Kenny's seat. "I appreciate that." With his left hand, Nick slides another $100 bill and a small bottle of OxyContin into Kenny's shirt pocket. As Kenny bends his head down to look in his pocket, Nick grabs the back of Kenny's neck with his right hand and turns Kenny's head to face him. "Don't blow it all in one place." He smiles. "Oh, and Kenny," he says, tightening his grip on Kenny's neck, "don't ever fuck with me. That would not be good. You understand that, right?"

"Hey, man. Of course. The pay's too good," Kenny adds tapping his shirt pocket. "I'm on your side all the way. Really. You just tell me what you need." Kenny very much wants to get out of Nick's van.

"Oh. I will." Nick fixes Kenny with a stare, he also holds his head in his large hand so that Kenny can feel his strong thumb on his throat just beneath his jaw. "Stay home tonight. I may need you later." He lets go and Kenny gets out of the car. "Don't forget."

Kenny is shaking as he walks away from the van. He thinks he might have peed in his pants. He has to stop and steady himself, and he puts his hand over his heart, over the $100 bill and the little bottle of OxyContin. He takes a deep breath. Then he becomes aware that Nick is watching him. When he hears the van start and the tires turn in the sand on the side road where they were parked, he braces for the sound of the engine racing. It doesn't come. Nick drives away slowly, not looking at him. Kenny exhales. "Fuck." He's sweating. He has definitely peed in his pants. But, as soon as he put his fingers back on the package in his shirt pocket, his heart rate begins to slow down. Just touching the package. He thinks maybe he'll do one now. He deserves it. Then he'll do one later.

Like a squirrel in the park who is terrified one moment and totally occupied with something else a moment later, Kenny heads for the High Rise where he can have a beer and take a hit and chill for a while. He might take them all this time and not give any to Jen. He didn't like having to tell Nick about Jen. It makes him angry with her. "Fuck her." His fear has morphed into defiance now that Nick is gone. He almost swaggers.

Then he sees the cop car pull in. It's an unmarked car, but Kenny knows every cop car marked or not. And he knows the detectives in this one: Petruzio and that little dick head

The Dead Woman in His Room

Henderson. He turns abruptly and walks over behind a tree. "Shit." The cop car pulls up next to Pete's van.

~~~

"Mr. Rangely," Petruzio calls over to Pete who is standing near the van with his uncle. He signals with his hand for Pete to approach the car. "We need to talk."

"Well, okay," Pete says, walking over to the car on Petruzio's side, "but can I just get my uncle upstairs to his apartment?"

"I've got a better idea" Petruzio said. "Officer Henderson here will escort your uncle to his room, and you can take his seat in the car, next to me."

"I don't know. My uncle is …"

"You want he should come to the station with us and wait there while we talk? You think he'd like that better? Your choice."

"Let me at least explain to him what you're going to do. Okay? He's got Alzheimer's and I don't want to upset him. He sometimes gets upset in the evenings."

"Yeah. You told me." Petruzio points to his lip. "The fat lip. I remember you said that. Actually, now I have an even better idea: let's all go up to your uncle's apartment, and we can talk there." Petruzio opens his car door and swings his feet out. "Then we'll all be comfortable. Besides, I've got some questions for your uncle, too." He shoves himself upright. Petruzio is obviously strong, even though he is also overweight.

"Don't you need a warrant or something," Pete is angry and feels obliged to object.

"Is that really going to be necessary?" Petruzio says leaning back against the car.

"No, I suppose not," Pete is trying to deflect his anger, so he won't act on it with the cops. "Stay for dinner. What the hell. I'm making spaghetti. You like spaghetti?"

"Let's talk first," Petruzio says pushing his door shut and walking over beside Pete. "I don't like to talk while I eat."

"Suit yourself."

The Dead Woman in His Room

Pete walks ahead and joins Willie. Petruzio and Henderson follow them into the High Rise.

~~~

Murph is on duty at the security desk and, when he sees Pete and his uncle with Petruzio and the short cop, he feels the same sense of conflict he felt when he told Petruzio that the woman who was killed on River Street had come to the High Rise and asked for Willie on the evening she was killed.

"I was the one who sent her to Mr. Rangely's room on River Street," Murph said. "It was at 9:32. I wrote it in my book. Pete must have got here with Willie after 10, because I would have told him, but Jeffrey was on duty, and he doesn't always read my notes."

Murph felt he had to report that piece of information to the cops as part of his duties as head of security at the High Rise. He hadn't told Pete about the woman, or his report to the cops, because Petruzio had asked him not to. Murph always does what he feels is required, but he feels uncomfortable about it this time because he likes Pete. Being part of any police investigation usually gives Murph a sense of importance, but this time it gives him a vague sense of betrayal. He would feel better if he could tell Pete what he had done. Murph only thinks in terms of right and wrong, and it confuses him when he does something right, but feels wrong about it. Seeing Pete and Willie and the two cops together recalls his dilemma.

"Hey, Murph. We're back for the evening," Pete calls over to him. "And we've got company. Do they need to sign in?" he adds in forced good humor.

"No, that's okay Pete. Thanks. I know Lt. Petruzio. I'll make a note."

Henderson breaks off from the group and approaches the security desk. "That's Lt. Petruzio and Detective Rick Henderson," he says, spelling out "H-E-N-D-E-R-S-O-N." He watches while Murph writes his name. Now that he's a real cop, Henderson feels vastly superior to security guards whose ranks he only recently left. When he turns back, he sees Petruzio glowering at him from inside the elevator. "You coming?"

Henderson rushes to join them just before the elevator doors close. No one speaks in the elevator.

~~~

This is the first time Pete has seen Petruzio since he was released from jail on the day after the murder. They didn't have enough evidence to charge him with anything. If Pete had called a lawyer, they wouldn't have even been able to keep him over night. Given the opportunity to make one call, however, Pete called Foxy. He didn't want her to hear about what happened on the news. He also didn't like lawyers much and, knowing his innocence, he counted on not needing one.

"We've learned a few things since we last spoke, Mr. Rangely." Petruzio says. They were sitting around the kitchen table in Willie's apartment. "Apparently, you have a trust fund, a rather significant trust fund."

"Yes. I have a trust fund," Pete says. "It was set up for me when I was 11 and my parents were killed in a car accident. It's a blind trust. It covered my school expenses, and I get a check every month, but I try not to depend on it. I don't even know how much is in it."

"There's actually quite a bit of money there," Petruzio says.

"You obviously know more about this than I do. Mind telling me what this has to do with anything?" Pete asks. "Lots of people have trust funds."

"Well. That's true. Lots of people do have trust funds—although I don't know anyone who does personally," he lets that thought hang in the air briefly. "But not many people have trust funds that are managed by women who turn up dead in their hotel rooms in Mill River. That's probably noteworthy, don't you think?"

The Dead Woman in His Room

Pete looks at Petruzio in disbelief. "I don't know what you're talking about. Are you telling me the woman who was killed in my room managed my trust fund?"

"Yes. In fact. That's what we have determined," Petruzio says.

"I never knew who managed that trust. I assumed it was something my parents or Willie set up for me." Pete looks at Willie who is expressionless. "This is news to me."

"Well. That is interesting, isn't it?"

"Not that interesting." Pete says. "I had no way of knowing who managed the trust. It's a blind trust. How did you even find this out?"

"A lot of secrets come out in a homicide investigation," Petruzio says. "We can open lots of doors. We also know that this Constance DeBreaux woman…did I tell you that was the name of the dead woman in your apartment…well it was. Anyway Ms. DeBreaux stopped here at the High Rise and spoke with Murph, the security guard. He's the one who told her where you lived. We know that because Murph told us. She asked for Willie here," indicating Willie as if he weren't really there. "So, you see, she obviously knew him, too. And then it turns out she managed a significant trust fund for you. Do you see how this is beginning to add up?"

"No."

"Well. Let me explain. You said that neither you nor you uncle had any connection to the dead woman in your apartment. That turns out not to be true; in either case. In fact, the late Ms. DeBreaux came to Mill River looking for your uncle Willie, so we know that she knew him. That's one thing. We also find that the late Ms. DeBreaux had control of your trust fund, your blind trust fund. That's two things. And, just today, we learned that control of your trust fund—which is worth in excess of $3 million by the way—would be handed over to you in the event that anything unfortunate—like turning up dead—happened to Ms. DeBreaux. That's three things. And you know what they add up to?"

Pete doesn't respond.

"That adds up to what we call motive," Petruzio says. "That's one of the three things we look for in a homicide investigation: motive, means and opportunity. We have established opportunity: you were alone with Ms. DeBreaux for at least 15 minutes before you called 911. We have a witness for that. Now, you see, we have motive: control of a $3 million trust fund. All we need is means and, Bingo, we have a case: Murder 1."

"But I didn't do this."

"That's right. You said that. And you had an alibi, too. You said you were with your uncle. This uncle," Petruzio points the index finger of his right hand at Willie so abruptly that Pete recoils slightly. Willie just sits there. "I remember you said that. And you said it was your uncle who gave you that nasty fat lip you had when I saw you later that night. But you know what's odd? The night clerk over at River Street remembers seeing you come in that evening, but he doesn't remember you having a fat lip. No one remembers you having a fat lip, until after the murder. And two people saw you: Murph over at the High Rise and Vinny, the night clerk at River Street. They don't remember a fat lip. Isn't that odd?"

Pete honestly doesn't know what to say. He can see how everything that evening could be interpreted exactly the way Petruzio has described it. He is thinking he must be in a dream, a bad dream.

"You know there's another thing that struck me as kind of odd," Petruzio says. "The room was a mess with your clothes thrown all over the place, but the dresser drawers were stacked up neatly on the bed. That seemed odd to me. I would have thought they'd have been thrown around, too."

"But that would make noise," Pete volunteers. "I thought about that, too."

"Is that why you stacked them? You wanted to make it look like someone had searched the room, but you didn't want to make any noise."

Pete puts his hands flat down on the table. "I didn't stack the drawers, lieutenant. I didn't kill anyone. I didn't know that woman, and I didn't know that my uncle knew her. There's a lot about my uncle that I will never know. He still surprises me." Pete looks at his uncle with concern but also obvious affection. "I don't know what to tell you…except it wasn't me. I didn't kill that woman."

"Then who did?"

Pete suddenly looks very concerned.

"Rangely?" Petruzio said, "You with us?"

Henderson, who has been following this dialogue without saying anything—under strict orders from Petruzio—reaches inside his jacket and puts his hand on his gun.

Pete shakes his head. "I just realized that if that woman knew my uncle, and if the man who killed her knew that she did, then the killer might come after my uncle."

"And why would that be?"

"I have no idea. I have no idea why anyone would want to hurt Willie."

"Oh, I don't know. Maybe," Petruzio held his palms up as if offering something. "Maybe … for the inheritance … just a thought. Your uncle has a trust fund, too. Didn't he tell you?"

Pete looks directly at Petruzio. "You've stacked everything up so in your mind it looks as if I killed that woman, but if you were so sure, you'd arrest me instead of sitting around here talking about it. You don't really know if I killed her or not. And if I didn't kill her, then there is a killer out there who might be coming after my uncle. Don't you get it? There must be somebody else."

"And who would that be?"

"How the hell should I know?"

"Maybe your uncle knows."

The Dead Woman in His Room

"That would be ironic, wouldn't it?" Pete says.

They all look at Willie. He doesn't look up.

"I think we're going to pass on your generous offer for dinner, tonight," Petruzio says pushing back from the table suddenly and standing up. He signals Henderson to get up, too. Henderson looks disappointed.

"Don't go anywhere, okay? We'll be back."

"I'm not going anywhere." Pete goes to the door and holds it open. "I'm not the killer, lieutenant. At least consider that possibility. That would change everything. You have to admit."

"Maybe." Petruzio says. "Maybe not."

As he walks toward the elevator, Petruzio is bothered by the fact that Pete might just be right. He hasn't given enough thought to the idea that the killer might be someone other than Pete. "Shit." He's starting to think like Henderson. He wishes he had a real partner, again. He feels very tired. Maybe he shouldn't wait for his wife Maureen to retire before he does. He never wanted to be one of those cops who just hangs on.

"He's the one," Henderson says as the elevator door closes in front of them. "You're right. I'm sure of it."

14

"I wish I had died before this night."

Pete stands behind the closed door for a while after the cops leave, absorbing the information they disclosed. Until that moment he was convinced that he had no association with the dead woman in his room. It was like some horrible accident that he had come upon but had nothing to do with. Now it appears the dead woman was involved in his life without his knowing about it since he was 11. How was that possible? Who was she?

And Willie. Uncle Willie, whom Pete had to admit he'd begun thinking of in the same vein as his old Golden Retriever Stony, Uncle Willie was apparently involved in some kind of real-life murder mystery. The dead woman, Constance something, had come to his apartment looking for Willie. Who was she to Willie and …

"Candice," Willie says suddenly. "They have killed my Candice."

Pete rushes back to the table and sits across from Willie. "What did you say? Who is Candice, Uncle Willie? And why would anyone kill her? What do you know about this?"

"Sweet, sad Candice. They have killed my Candice."
"Who? Who killed Candice?"
"HAL."
"Who?"

"HAL. It must be HAL; after all these years." Tears are running down Willie's face, but he just sits there motionless, as if he can't process the emotions that his memory has unleashed.

"Who is Hal, Uncle Willie? And what do you know about this? Please try to remember. It's very important. Was Hal a friend of yours? Why would he kill Candice? Please, Uncle Willie. Please remember."

Willie gets up from the table and Pete figures he has learned everything he is going to from Uncle Willie that night. Moving slowly, almost robot-like, Willie makes his way across the living room to where his saxophone case is stacked on top of his old PA system. The pile of music gear is like a shrine in his apartment for a God Willie's forgotten. He never goes to it, but he did make it clear that he didn't want anyone else touching any of it. Pete remembers his blunder when he opened the case without asking one time.

Willie opens the case and takes out the saxophone with one hand while he hangs the strap around his neck with the other. Moving slowly, he hooks the strap onto the horn and tests its weight as he must have done ten thousand times in the past.

"My God. He's going to play," Pete thinks, watching as Willie opens the bottom of the case where the mouthpiece was kept. But Willie doesn't take out the mouthpiece. Instead, he holds the case with his left hand and reaches down with his right and, after feeling around with his fingers, rips the fabric out of the bottom of the case. Pete hears the tearing sound of Velcro strips coming apart. He is too fascinated to do anything but watch. Folding the red fabric in both hands, Willie pushes it back into a corner of the case and then reaches in and pulls out a document. Carrying the document, with the saxophone still hanging around his neck, still without the mouthpiece, Willie approaches Pete.

"This. This is why they killed my Candice. She told me. She warned me." He hands Pete the document. He looks at Pete. "I wish I had died before this night," he says. Then he sits at the table with the saxophone hanging around his neck.

As much as Pete wants to look at the document in his hands, he can't keep from staring at his uncle as he sits with tears running down his cheeks. Pete is struck by how little he really knows about his uncle. He is struck as well by the depth of his uncle's sense of loss. He is afraid for him. He is afraid the moment of clarity that Willie just experienced will be too much for him to bear.

Slowly, Pete's attention is drawn back to the document he holds in his hands. It's a handwritten letter to Willie, dated four years ago. He reads the letter to himself, not sure what the impact of his reading it out loud could have on Willie.

> Dear Willie,
>
> I don't know if I will ever be able to tell you this in person, so I will attempt to write it down for you here in this letter. You have not only a right to know this, but you may also one day have a need to know.
>
> You are perhaps the one honest person I ever met, and I have betrayed you. Kyle and I betrayed you by involving you in HAL Holdings in Denver in 1978.
>
> HAL Holdings was a scam. I can say that of all the different financial schemes that Kyle and I were involved in over the years of our partnership, this was the only one that was unabashedly illegal.
>
> You may remember that Denver was in the throes of an energy boom when we were there, and money was everywhere. In that environment, we told investors that HAL Holdings was a private offshore bank in the Cayman Islands, and we billed it as the perfect place to hide money from the IRS, investors, business partners, wives, ex-wives, you name it. I'm not particularly proud of it, but we only took deposits from unethical businessmen; I used my

adoptive father as the model. I suppose it was a kind of getting even. You may remember meeting a sleazy lawyer named Nick Barons. He directed depositors to us. He did other kinds of dirty work for most of them. And he was a depositor himself.

In the end, we took a lot of money from a relatively small group of men who were so full of themselves that they could justify anything that suited their ends. It was their capacity to justify their own misappropriation of funds, in fact, that drove them to pour money into HAL Holdings. They were so willing to believe that whatever they did was smart that we could have told them anything.

I have to say I feel no remorse for taking money from these men. Kyle and I were both sickened by the stories of where all the money was coming from. These weren't criminals, per se. That made it all the worse in some ways. It was as if we had struck a gusher of greed in the Denver boom; and it flowed all over us. Any satisfaction that we might have taken from the success of HAL was so tainted by their sordid little stories that, in the end, all we wanted to do was stop the flow and cover it up.

There was no reason to involve you in any of this, but Kyle insisted that you play a role. You may remember playing at the dinner party when we closed the fund. I did not want to involve you in this in any way, but I did not stop it from happening, and I'm not even sure I could if I tried. I did not realize the depth of Kyle's need to impress you. I knew Kyle didn't love me. But I did not realize until then that he loved you.

Pete can't help looking up at his uncle in amazement.

The Dead Woman in His Room

And I know that you did not know. How little we know about each other!

Neither of us ever really needed the money. It wasn't so much about money. Honestly, I'm not sure what it was about. I still had a lot of anger and Kyle had a lot of ego. Maybe it was about that.

Anyway. We folded HAL Holdings and left Denver in the late '70s. Kyle and I had built HAL Holdings out of smoke and mirrors and a logo, so it was relatively easy to make it disappear without a trace. We had all the money in numbered accounts in a Swiss Bank: one account for each of us, including you.

It wasn't that hard to disappear. We walked away from everything in Denver, booked flights to the Cayman Islands, and picked up new identities there. That's when I became Constance DeBreaux, and Kyle became Shamus Bourne. I also used my knowledge of computer systems to obscure any links to you. And we never looked back. Actually, I looked back. I wanted to see if anyone was on our trail. There never was. The money that was deposited in HAL wasn't supposed to exist in the first place, so no one was in a position to report it stolen. They had no legal recourse. I read in the Denver papers that Nick Barons was found dead on his ranch in Nederland, but I never read anything about HAL Holdings.

There may never be anyone on our trail. It's been a long time now and it seems less likely all the time that anyone could connect any of us to HAL. I'm not really telling you because I think you need to know. I'm telling you because I need to tell you. I feel I owe you that.

Meeting you changed my life. Just knowing there was someone like you forced to me to accept that not all men were like my adoptive father. You were the first truly decent man I ever met, and, frankly, I haven't met many others.

It may not have occurred to you over the years, but I've thought often about what kind of relationship we might have had if I was more to you than just the friend of Kyle's who managed your accounts. I guess I still wonder sometimes.

The money is still there, and it has grown significantly. Kyle and I agreed to make you a one-third partner. Your share was $8,768,453.87 on the last statement. I used some to open the trust fund for your nephew and a couple of times I replenished your savings accounts when they got low. I don't think you even noticed. I know it was important to you to make your living as a musician, and you always had the investments Kyle made for you to tide you over. You never were much of a spender.

I guess I've been remiss as your financial planner for not telling you about this sooner. Selfishly, I didn't want to tell you because it was like admitting to a lie. Maybe I was afraid you'd fire me, and I wanted to have at least that connection to you. I don't know why. It's not like me. I just didn't.

Anyway. The money is in Crédit Lyonnais in Zurich and your account number is 8367993. The security code that you will need to access the account is 7710943. They may also ask you a security question. Whatever the question, the answer is the word "goodbye." If anything happens to either Kyle or me, the money in our accounts will accrue to yours.

So now you know. I guess I feel better for having written this — although I still haven't mailed it. I'd rather tell you this in person, but I'm not sure I can.

The Dead Woman in His Room

The letter just ends. It's not signed. Pete looks through the pages to see if he missed the last of it, and the signature.

"This letter is not signed, Willie. It just stops." Pete looks across the table at his uncle, who didn't move at all while he read. "This is from Constance…or Candice, isn't it?"

After a moment Willie says, "Yes. She came to New York, and she told me. And then she gave me this letter. That was the last time I saw her." Willie pauses.

Pete looks at his uncle and is overwhelmed. He doesn't know what to say. Then he's jolted by a realization: "That's what you meant, isn't it? You said HAL killed Candice. This all has to do with HAL Holdings, doesn't it? The killer is someone who deposited money in HAL Holdings. But that would make him as old as you. That doesn't make sense."

Pete looks over at his uncle. "Are you okay? Willie. Do you want to lie down? Let me put your horn away." Pete stands up and gently unhooks the saxophone from around Willie's neck. Before putting it away, he lines up the Velcro under the red liner in the bottom of the case and carefully sets the horn in its place and snaps the latches. He can see when he gets back to the table that Willie's moment of clarity is over. The expression has gone out of his face. Maybe that's a good thing.

"I'm going to make you some dinner, Willie. Spaghetti." Pete says. "Why don't you just relax. I'll put on some music. How about Stanley Turrentine? I know you like Turrentine."

Pete's mind is racing. He always thought his uncle had an interesting life; but not this interesting. Offshore banking scams, Swiss bank accounts with millions of dollars, a man who was in love with him; the woman who wrote this letter was obviously in love with him.

Pete exhales abruptly. The image of the dead woman in his room on River Street flashes before him. The woman with the deep slash on her cheek and the blood everywhere, lying on the floor with his clothes strewn over her and her skirt hiked up.

The Dead Woman in His Room

That was her. That was the woman who wrote the letter he had just read.

The dead woman had been just a horrible image. Now she's a person, an interesting person, a person who loved his uncle. A person he might have known. He felt her death suddenly at a visceral level. The image of her becomes so clear in his mind, he can see that she was still bleeding when he found her. She must have only just died. He doesn't feel faint, exactly. He feels as if he is dissipating, dissolving into the room. He becomes aware of his hands in front of him still holding the pot on the stove. It's as if they aren't his hands.

The feeling passes. It's followed by the certainty, that whoever killed that woman is out there, and that Willie could very well be his next target. But who could it be?

Pete reads the letter again and then folds it and puts it in his back pocket.

~~~

Nick sees the cops leave. He doesn't need Kenny to tell him they are cops. He can always tell cops. Nick is back in the shadows near enough to the High Rise where he can watch the building.

He's getting increasingly impatient. The sense of calm that he always feels when he's stalking someone for a hit is not available to him in this case. On another case, he could wait for days without impatience, waiting for just the right moment to strike. That kind of waiting increased the certainty of his success. Waiting to kill someone, he could almost stop himself from breathing like some kind of Indian holy man. This kind of waiting makes him crazy. He knows he can't kill Willie or the trail to HAL Holdings will be completely lost. He doesn't know what to do. He hates that feeling.

It occurs to him that if he had somebody who means something to this Willie guy, maybe then he could swap him for the information he needs. The nephew, Pete, could be that somebody. Pete could even have the information he needs. The assholes could already be living on his money.

This could work. He's seen Pete go into the High Rise with Willie. Kenny pointed him out. He remembers him. He'll wait for Pete to come out, and then he'll grab him. But he won't kill him right away. He'll find out what he knows. Then he can use him as a hostage. He can use him to buy back the money his father stole from him. The thought of his father has him wringing his hands on the steering wheel as he sits staring at the doors to the High Rise.

Nick sits that way for a long time. It's quiet. Few people come and go from the High Rise after dark. The windows glow with the blue glare of televisions. A chill fall wind stalks the grounds, stopping and starting, scurrying through the leaves, part hiding, part looking. There are no stars.

15

"The police are coming!"

"Where the fuck were you all afternoon?" Kenny barks.

"I don't know what you're talking about?" Jen says. "What do you care what I do anyway?"

They're standing in the kitchen in their apartment on the 5th floor of the High Rise. Jen is putting away some groceries. At five foot two, she is about three inches shorter than Kenny. Jen wears an extra-large black T-shirt that says "Queen Gaga" on the front. It hangs slightly off one shoulder and drapes halfway to her knees. She keeps adjusting it on her shoulders, but each time she reaches up with her right arm to put something in the cupboards, the shirt slips off her left shoulder. It's not particularly sexy. Jen is not particularly sexy. Although she once was. She looks tired most of the time now. Her high cheek bones make her face look taught. She's been losing weight since Kenny moved in with her. Jen has short brown hair, spiked on the right side of her head. It was dyed purple on the ends, but not recently. It looks rinsed out. Jen looks rinsed out. Kenny has been helping himself to half of the Oxy she was prescribed after she hurt her back stocking shelves at Walmart; and her half isn't enough. She was on food stamps before Walmart laid her off. Now she's on disability as well. It's not enough.

Fresh from his encounter with Nick, Kenny is overcompensating for his episode of abject terror by acting macho with Jen. Jen is being uncharacteristically non-compliant, and it causes Kenny to get louder and more aggressive. He's already taken one of the Oxys, and he's feeling no pain. He's feeling mean; he wants to hurt something.

"I saw you hanging out with the old ladies. They your friends now? You in a hurry to get like them?"

Jen puts a package of Ramen next to the stove. "Fuck you Kenny. I can go where I want. I don't have to ask your permission. You don't own me."

Kenny isn't used to Jen talking back to him like this. He tries another tack.

"I'm doing some business with a guy who wants information on your new best friends: Pete and Willie. They're not so squeaky clean, you know. I know what they're into."

Jen turns away from the cupboards and looks at Kenny for the first time. "You don't know shit, Kenny. You never did."

"Yeah. Well, you better stay away from them. This guy I'm doing business with is one scary motherfucker. I think it's a mob thing."

"What are you talking about … mob thing? Pete and Willie. You're delirious. You've got delusions of grandeur. Are you smoking crack again?"

"I'm tellin' ya. It's gotta be the mob. It's something dirty. The guy pays me in $100 bills." Kenny pulls his most recent payment out of his shirt pocket. "See." He holds it up in front of her with both hands, pressing it into her face. "See. See!"

She bats his hands away and, in the process, tears the bill in half.

He looks at the halves in each hand in disbelief.

"Look what you did!" he shrieks. "You ripped it. You bitch."

"Fuck you, Kenny." Jen is yelling now too. "It's probably fake, anyway. Just like you. Everything about you is fake, fake, fake."

"I'll show you fake," Kenny yells back, putting the halves of his torn bill in his pocket.

The Dead Woman in His Room

He slaps her hard across the face. The slap makes a loud smacking sound – loud enough for Ralph to hear on the other side of the wall in his living room. He hears them shouting.

Ralph has heard them shouting at each other before, and each time he dreads hearing the sound of them actually hitting each other. Just shouting he could ignore. But hitting. He dreads the prospect of having to intervene. He doesn't want to hear any hitting. He doesn't think he can ignore hitting. At least he doesn't want to think he can.

Usually a slap is the end of it.

Jen stares back at Kenny. Angry at her tears as much as the pain on her cheek. She rocks back against the kitchen counter.

"No more, Kenny. I'm not taking this shit from you anymore." She reaches out blindly with her right hand, grabs a plate off the counter, and swings it at Kenny. It bounces off his shoulder and falls on the floor.

Ralph hears it break.

Kenny is stunned. Jen never hit back. He slaps her again and her head bounces back into the cupboards. Ralph hears the slap and the impact of her head hitting the cupboards.

Jen swings back blindly.

Kenny punches her in the face. This is a different sound. Not as loud but harder. Ralph hears the sound. He hears Jen cry out from the pain.

Jen sweeps her arm along counter and scoops everything onto the floor between her and Kenny. Ralph hears the plates fall and break.

Kenny punches her in the stomach, and Ralph hears Jen grunt from the force. She doubles over.

"Stop that!" Ralph yells at the wall, not very loud.

Still doubled over, Jen punches out and hits Kenny in the balls. Ralph hears Kenny yell out in pain and surprise.

"Stop that!" Ralph yells at the wall, a little louder.

Jen stands up first and backs into the counter holding her stomach. Kenny lets go of his balls and dives at her. Ralph hears them slam against the counter. They are both yelling.

Ralph starts yelling, "Stop that. Stop that." He's pacing back and forth on the other side of the wall. "Stop it." The Thorazine in his system makes his arms rise up involuntarily from his sides giving him the appearance of a deranged crane honking at the wall.

Jen pushes at Kenny with all her might, and he slips on the broken glass and falls on the floor. Ralph hears the thud.

Then he hears when Kenny grabs Jen's legs and pulls them out from under her. Ralph hears her fall.

"Stop it! Stop it!" he yells at the wall. "I'm going to call the police," Ralph looks across the room for his phone. "I'm calling the police," he yells, but he seems unable to tear himself away from his place in front of the wall and get to his phone.

He hears thrashing on the floor on the other side of the wall. And screaming. Both of them. Obscenities and screams blurring into each other. He hears the kicking and pounding as Kenny and Jen roll back and forth in their violent embrace. They kick at each other and hit the cupboards, making the doors slam and bounce open; again and again.

"I'm calling the police. I'm calling the police," Ralph yells. He runs across the room, grabs his phone, and carries it back to the wall, as if he wants them to be able to see what he's doing. "I'm calling the police. I'm calling 911." Ralph is yelling now, too.

Ralph lowers his voice when the emergency operator answers. "They're fighting. It's terrible. I can hear them. Room 505. In the High Rise. Yes. I'll stay on the line, but hurry. I think he's killing her. I've never heard anything like this before."

"I called the police," Ralph yells at the wall. "The police are coming." Knowing that the operator can hear him makes Ralph self-conscious. He cups his hand over the phone. "The police are on their way," he says to the wall professorially. Then louder, "The police are coming. You better stop."

On the other side of the wall, oblivious to Ralph's plaintive calls, Kenny and Jen are exhausting themselves in their frenzy. Jen is as strong as Kenny, but not as vicious. Lying on his side, kicking, and yelling, he punches her in the breast. He punches her in the side. Jen finally puts her hands over her head and curls into a fetal position on the broken glass, trying to protect herself.

Kenny clambers to his feet and kicks her. The kick drives Jen into the counter with a crash and causes Kenny to stumble and fall back against the table. He throws the heavy glass ash tray. It misses Jen and crashes into the wall scattering cigarette butts and ash everywhere. To Ralph the ash tray hitting the wall sounds like a hammer blow. Then he hears Kenny yelling from further down the wall. Kenny has grabbed a chair, and he hurls it into the kitchen. Ralph hears it bounce off the wall and hit the floor. It misses Jen. She isn't moving now. She's just lying on the floor, curled up tight with her arms over her head.

Kenny is yelling. He's in the living room, now, ranting, and raving and throwing whatever item happens to come to his attention. Ralph follows the sound down his wall, holding the phone in front of him as if the emergency operator could hear what he hears.

"The police are coming," Ralph yells. "The police are coming."

Kenny doesn't hear a thing. He's so caught up in his fury, looking for more things to throw. By now much of the furniture is piled in front of Jen. He can't really hit her anymore. He throws magazines, he starts to throw the coffee table, but it's too heavy for him. He throws more ash trays and a lamp, even a sofa seat. He just grabs and throws and yells and curses and kicks his way like a dervish through the apartment toward the door.

With Ralph pacing him on the other side of the wall, still holding the phone up to the wall. "The police are coming. The police are coming," he repeats. He's made it almost the full length of his living room wall and is standing in front of the door to the hallway. He hears Kenny yank the door open so hard it slams into the wall. Ralph can feel the force through the floor. Kenny staggers into the hallway, still yelling curses.

Ralph pauses slightly before he unlocks the illegal deadbolt he installed on his front door. He gets his door open just in time to see Kenny entering the stairwell, the door bounces back when he pushes it in front of him and almost knocks him down as he staggers forward.

"The police are coming," Ralph yells after him, still holding in the phone in front of him. "The police are coming."

The silence after Kenny leaves traps Ralph in the hall. Mrs. Peterson has opened her door and looks out inquisitively.

"The police are coming," he tells her. Ralph is standing outside the door to Jen's apartment. The door is part way open, and he can see the result of Kenny's violence. The place looks as if it has been ransacked. Ralph wants to rush in and see if Jen is all right. He wants to do the right thing.

He just can't.

Ralph is standing there holding his phone when Marge rushes past him into the apartment. She heard the call come in on the police band radio: "Code 1. Domestic violence at the High Rise. Apartment 505." She knew immediately.

Ralph stands in the hall and looks in as Marge makes her way deeper into the apartment, pushing things out of the way to get to Jen.

~~~

Nick sees Kenny burst out of the building. He's moving like an animated stick figure, arms and legs flapping as if the strings that hold all the pieces together have been stretched.

Something's up. Nick hears police sirens in the distance.

Kenny hears the sirens, too. He knows they are coming for him. This is bad. This is very bad. He veers by some shrubbery and Nick can see him deposit something in the bush. He pushes it deep down inside.

Then he steps back into the High Rise driveway just as the cops pull in. Kenny never runs from cops. He has a terror of being shot. Besides he knows all the cops, and they already know he is willing to do whatever they want to make things easy on him. There is no reason to resist.

He's also hurt. Jen connected more than a few times. Bitch. As he gently explores his various sores with his hand, he feels a comforting rush of moral outrage. It wasn't all his fault. He could tell them that.

The cops drive up directly in front of him. Kenny cups his hands over his face to shade his eyes from the headlights.

"Kenny, Kenny, Kenny," he hears the driver say. He knows immediately who it is. Kenny peers over the lights into the car. It's Marge's son Patrick and his partner Roxanne Mangalusi. He went to high school with her. He knows some things about her from those days that weren't very cop-like. Patrick was a couple of years ahead of them in school. Kenny steps over to the driver's side door.

"So, Kenny," Patrick says. "We hear there's been a problem. Know anything about that?"

"What problem. No problem here. Just going out for a walk."

"Well, Kenny. You're going to have to postpone your walk. We're going to have to go back inside. You just stand there with Roxanne while I park the car."

Roxanne appears from behind the car. She looks good in her cop's uniform, Kenny thinks. He just stands there. "Anything you say. Always willing to cooperate with the police. You know me." Kenny affects an air of camaraderie and looks Roxanne up and down as she walks toward him.

"Looks like you fell down, Kenny," Roxanne says, looking Kenny up and down in return. "You should be more careful. Looks like you wet your pants, too," she adds.

The Dead Woman in His Room

Kenny turns away and looks down at the ground. Patrick comes up on the other side of him and they walk together into the High Rise. Kenny limps to exaggerate his injuries.

Nick watches. After a few minutes he walks along the shadows over to the bush where Kenny stopped. Tucked inside is the small bottle of OxyContin he gave Kenny earlier. It's been opened. Nick puts it into this pocket and steps back into the darkness to wait. Now he knows Kenny will be back.

~~~

The door is open, and all the lights are on in Jen's apartment when Kenny and the two cops arrive. They haven't spoken on the way up. Neither of the cops expect Jen to press charges. She never has. They're all just going through the motions.

Jen and Marge are sitting together on the sofa. Marge put two of the three seat cushions back for them. She left everything else where it was. Marge has a washcloth and is dabbing at some cuts that Jen has on her head.

"Don't want there to be any glass left in there," she says, adding, "These look clean. You'll be all right."

"Ma!" Marge's son exclaims when he walks in. "We're going to have to put you on the payroll if you keep getting to crime scenes ahead of us."

He looks around the apartment. "Wow. This place is a mess. You outdid yourself, Kenny. How's she?"

"She's fine," Marge says. "She's just banged up."

"Who wants to tell us what happened here?" Patrick says. "Not you, ma. One of these two." He takes Kenny by the shoulder and sits him down in a chair across from the couch.

"We just had a little disagreement," Kenny says. "And it kinda got out of hand. You know how that goes."

"No, I don't, Kenny. Tell me."

"We were arguing over money," Kenny says. "That's what couples do, isn't it? It's hard to make ends meet these days. Pay the bills. Pay the rent. Nothin' left."

Jen glowers at Kenny. Her nose is running and the red marks on her face are starting to turn to bruises.

"Is that what this was about Jen? Money?"

Jen takes a deep breath. "Yeah. Sure. That's what it was about. Money. I guess that's what this was about."

"Who started this?"

"It just kind of happened," Kenny says. "Didn't it? Jen. I think one of us slipped and bumped into the other. Isn't that how you remember it, Jen?"

"Let us ask the questions, Kenny."

"Are you going to press charges, this time Jen? This can't be a whole lot of fun for you. You know we've been here before, but we can't do anything if you won't press charges."

"Hey, that's entrapment," Kenny objects, "or something."

"Shut up, Kenny. Just sit there and don't talk."

Patrick walks over and looks down at Jen. "Your choice, Jen. You don't have to let this happen over and over again."

"Yeah, right," Jen sniffs hard. "That's gonna change."

Marge puts her arm around Jen's shoulder and looks up at her son.

"Can't you just get him out of here for a while? She's been through enough tonight. Just keep him away from here as long as you can. Maybe you can drop him down a flight of stairs," she adds matter-of-factly.

Kenny looks suspiciously at Patrick.

Patrick looks down at the two women on the couch. "Ma. I swear I'm going to arrest you one of these days for interfering with police work."

"Just take him out of here," Marge says waving her hand like a dust broom. "Take him for a long ride. Maybe you can talk some sense into him."

Kenny takes a step back.

The Dead Woman in His Room

Patrick grabs Kenny's right arm. "Better come with us, Kenny, or I'm going to let ma talk some sense into you herself. You don't want that, trust me."

Patrick stops in the doorway. "I'm going to leave this door ajar" he says. "The ambulance guys should be here any time. Actually, they should've been here by now. I don't know what's keeping those guys. Feels like it's going to be a busy night," he adds more or less to himself as he follows Kenny into the hall.

~~~

"Kenny's into something bad," Jen tells Marge after the cops take Kenny away. "I don't know what it is, but he's involved with someone really scary. He's way over his head this time. I can tell."

"Is that what you were fighting over?" Marge asks.

"I don't know what we were fighting over. We just fight. We always have." Jen blows her nose hard. "You know what's weird. Kenny said whatever he's involved in has something to do with Pete and Willie." Remembering more of the details, she adds, "This guy's paying him for information about Pete and Willie. He has a $100 bill the guy gave him, just today. A hundred dollars! That doesn't make any sense to me at all."

It made a little sense to Marge. Marge knew more about the dead woman who was found in Pete's room than most. Some of it she got from reading between the lines on what was said on the police band radio. Some of what she knew she got from her son. He refused to tell her much, but she did find out that the dead woman had come to see Willie at the High Rise before she went to Pete's apartment.

Marge's son probably got his investigative sense from his mother. What her son didn't have was her complete and utter confidence in her ability to judge someone's character. As far as Marge is concerned, Pete is innocent. She has no question in her mind about that. And Willie…what could he be involved in? This scary guy Jen was talking about; Marge realizes he could be the killer. He must still be around.

The Dead Woman in His Room

The ambulance crew arrives with a gurney, and they insist that Jen go to the hospital for observation. After they leave, Marge hurries back to her apartment. She wants to call Pete as soon as possible. Later Patrick would want to know why she hadn't called him first with this information, but that would be much later.

~~~

Patrick and his partner Roxanne drive Kenny around in the patrol car for a half-hour or so until the ridiculousness of the situation makes it impossible for them to keep him any longer. They aren't either of them the kind of cops who could convincingly put the fear of God, much less police brutality, in anyone. Mostly, they want him out of their car. Kenny attempts to ingratiate himself by talking about their time in high school together, as if they had all been friends. The idea is offensive to both of them. Patrick is also uncomfortable with the thought that he's acting on orders from his mom while he's on duty.

During his time in the backseat of the patrol car, Kenny thinks briefly about telling the cops about Nick, but he can tell he's already off the hook for this situation, and he doesn't want to spend that bit of information until he can buy something much bigger with it.

"Go home, Kenny," Patrick says through the grate on the back of the seat in the patrol car. "But let me tell you something, Kenny, if we get called back here on account of you, for any reason, I'll press charges myself. And you won't just go for a ride around town then, Kenny. You'll go away. Do you understand what I'm telling you?"

"Of course," Kenny says, he's feeling cocky, like he's gotten away with something—his highest goal in life.

Patrick gets out of the car and opens the back door to let Kenny out.

"Oh, and Kenny," he adds as Kenny stands up next to him. "I'll make sure that everyone where you'll be going knows you're a snitch. They might want to arrange a special kind of welcome for you. You know how much they like snitches on the inside. Think about it."

Kenny staggers when he takes his first step, and it causes him to lurch forward away from the car.

"I may have something for you," Kenny says, "something big."

"Sure Kenny," Patrick says. "Save it. You may need it."

~~~

Kenny watches the car pull out of the driveway. He is comforted somewhat by the darkness that it left behind. Then he remembers the little bottle of Oxy that he stashed in the bushes on his way out. That's what he needs. He starts to feel a little better. He looks around to see if anyone is nearby and slinks over to the bush.

He almost reaches it when Nick steps out from behind a tree. "Looking for these?" he says, shaking the bottle so the pills rattle inside.

Kenny jumps back. "Jesus, man. You scared me. I was lookin' for you."

"Yeah. Uh huh." Nick glares at him, turning the pill bottle over and over in his hands. "What were you doing with the police, Kenny?"

"Oh. That was nothin'. I got in a fight. I hit the old lady, and somebody called the cops. It was nothing. They just drove me around the block a few times, trying to act tough. They don't scare me."

"You should always be afraid of the police," Nick says. "I am."

"You! I didn't think you were afraid of anything."

"No. Kenny. I am afraid of the police. And I am afraid of anybody who is not afraid of the police. That means I'm a little afraid of you right now Kenny. I'm not sure we can work together anymore." Nick starts to put the pill bottle in his jacket pocket.

"Hey, come on, man."

"What can you do for me now, Kenny?" Nick says.

"I know things."

"What things, Kenny?" Nick starts to walk toward Kenny. "What things can you tell me?"

Kenny is backing up. Nick still turns the bottle of pills over in his hand. Kenny can hear the pills rattle inside the bottle. "The cops. I overheard them in the car. They're going to arrest that guy Pete for the murder of the woman on River Street. No one knows that," he adds to give it some extra value. "One of the detectives is real hot to do that tonight. That's useful right?"

"Why is that useful? You think I had something to do with that woman? Is that what you think Kenny?" Nick is very close now.

"No man. I never thought that, honest. Why would I think that? I just thought having the cops take that guy Pete away might interfere with your plans. I thought you would want to know that. That's why I was looking for you."

Kenny is actually pretty good at stringing circumstances together, so they serve his purposes...even when he is scared, especially when he is scared. "That's useful right?"

That was useful. Nick knows that Pete wasn't involved in the murder, but having the cops take him away could delay everything. It could certainly make it more complicated. On the other hand, it occurs to him that if he takes Pete out now, the cops might even be more convinced that Pete murdered the woman. That could be useful. The cops could think he's making a run for it. Then, if Pete turns up dead, they might not look any further. Nick knows cops quickly lose interest in solving the murder of a murderer. One less bad guy for the system to put back on the streets. That's how they think. He knows that. That's what they thought when his sister was shot off her motorcycle. "Good riddance."

Nick seems so engrossed in his thoughts that Kenny thinks for a split second about running away. Then he thinks better of it.

"I could get you in there," he says. "I know all the ways in and out. I worked in there one time, in maintenance. I know every closet. I know the security, too. Yeah, man. I know the security. I know where the cameras are, the little room with the monitors. I know where they keep the keys."

"Shut up."

Kenny stops.

16

*"Don't let anything else happen before
I get there."*

Pete doesn't hear the phone ring until just before the answering machine picks up. He was going to let the machine take a message, but when he hears Marge's voice saying, "Pete, Pete, are you in there? It's Marge. Pick up. It's very important," he grabs the phone.

"Marge. It's Pete. What's up? I'm kind of busy…"

"I think the real killer is here."

"What!? What killer? What are you talking about?"

"I can't tell you everything that has happened on the phone, but Jen just told me that someone has been paying Kenny to spy on you and your uncle. I think you should get out of that apartment immediately."

Pete turns involuntarily to look at the door. As usual, he's left it ajar in case Ralph or Bud happen by. He goes over and shuts the door with his foot.

"How do you know about all of this?" Pete asks.

"My son's a cop, remember. He told me the dead woman had come to the High Rise to see Willie before going to your apartment."

Pete is taken aback by Marge's matter-of-fact statement and looks at the phone in his hand in disbelief. He is amazed by all the information other people seem to have about his life. He's always the observer. It hadn't occurred to him that he is also observed. It seems significant, on some level.

"Pete!" Marge's voice brings him back. "I think you should bring your uncle here to my apartment. He'll be safe. No one will think to look for him here."

"You're right, Marge. I'll bring Willie right down. I just need to call Foxy first."

"Don't be too long," Marge says, but Pete has already hung up and is dialing Foxy's number.

~~~

When Pete calls, Foxy is at her kitchen table. She lets the answering machine take the call so she can find out who it is before answering.

"Foxy. It's Pete. Are you there?"

Foxy brightens, "Hi. Where are you?"

"I'm still at the High Rise. It's been quite an evening. The police were here. They're convinced I killed that woman."

"You're kidding me."

"I wish. That's just the beginning. The police also told me that the woman who was killed came to the High Rise to see Willie before going to my room at River Street."

"She knew Willie?"

"Get this. She not only knew Willie. She knew me. According to the cops she is the one who has been managing my trust fund all these years; the one that was set up when my parents died. She set that up. Constance DeBreaux was a fake name. Her real name was Candice Bergeron."

"But…?"

"There's more: Back in the late '70s she and Willie and guy named Kyle were involved in some kind of banking scam. Something called HAL Holdings. Apparently they stole money from a bunch of sleazy businessmen. Willie had a letter…yeah this is amazing. Willie had a letter hidden in the bottom of his saxophone case. It was from Candice apologizing for involving him in their banking scam. She was obviously in love with Willie. There are codes and passwords in the letter for an account in a Swiss private bank that apparently belongs to Willie. It's got millions in it. Willie's rich."

"You know what though…I hadn't told Willie about the woman in my room, but he was there when the cops were talking about it. And he understood who they were talking about. He was crying after they left. You know what he said to me; he said, 'I wish I had died before this night.' I think he was really clear at that moment. That's when he went over to his horn case and pulled this letter out of a secret compartment. It tells the whole story. I felt so bad for him. What a way to find out something like that. He's in the bathroom now. I think he's lost it again. I almost hope so, for his sake. Must be like waking up into a nightmare, instead of the other way around. I'm going to take him to Marge's apartment."

"Why Marge's?"

"Whew. Another long story. Marge just called and told me that Jen's husband Kenny is being paid to spy on me and Willie. He had a $100 bill in his pocket that he got from this guy tonight. Marge says she think he's the killer. I don't know who he is, but he's here; and he obviously knows where Willie lives. Willie will be safe at Marge's for now."

"I'm coming over."

"No, that's not necessary."

"Yeah. Right. I'll meet you at Marge's in ten minutes. Don't let anything else happen before I get there. I'm serious."

"Okay." Pete pauses. He almost says, "I love you."

She almost says, "I love you, too."

A lot is going on.

~ ~ ~

By the time Foxy shows up, Marge's apartment has the feel of a war room except, instead of young soldiers in uniform, it's filled with old ladies. Marge's friend Anna is there, and Gretchen.

The Dead Woman in His Room

Ralph and Bud are also there. The two men look uncomfortably out of place. The atmosphere isn't exactly feminine, but it is definitely female. The two men sit on either side of Willie who is seated on the couch staring into space.

Marge and Pete are talking when Foxy arrives.

"She's going to be all right," Marge is saying.

"Who's going to be all right?" Foxy asks, walking up to them.

"Jen." Marge says.

"Kenny beat her up," Pete says.

"When did this happen?"

"Just a while ago. That's when Marge found out from Jen that Kenny is spying on us."

"Did anyone call the police?" Foxy asks, sitting down next to Pete at the kitchen table.

"Yeah, our man Ralph here." Pete says loud enough so Ralph can hear him. "Ralph's the hero of the night. He heard Jen and Kenny fighting next door and called the cops."

Pete continues in a lower voice, "Kenny ran away, but the police picked him up outside. He's with them now. It was Marge's son, Patrick."

"Which cops did you talk to? Foxy asks," turning to Pete.

"Petruzio and his sidekick Henderson."

"Now I'm confused," Marge says to Pete. "You didn't tell me they were here."

"Yeah. I didn't get to that. They came to tell me I killed the woman in my apartment."

Pete glances at Foxy. She understands that Pete has not told Marge everything he told her.

"That's ridiculous," Marge says, jumping up. "I'm going to call my son, right now. And I have half a mind to call Dominick and tell that big jerk that he's barking up the wrong tree. I knew him when he was walking a beat." Marge turns away from the table and sets off for her telephone.

The Dead Woman in His Room

"So, tell me about this guy who's paying Kenny to spy on you. What do you know about him" Foxy asks.

"Not much, unfortunately."

The small size of the table makes Pete and Foxy sit close to each other. It makes them both a little uneasy, as if they're keeping a secret from everyone…but they're not sure what it is.

They turn away and look around the kitchen.

Anna is at the stove cooking perogies—every event calls for perogies as far as Anna is concerned.

Gretchen is crouched in the corner, sketching on one the pads Pete has given her.

Pete leans toward Gretchen.

"You're out on the grounds a lot, Gretchen. Have you seen Kenny with anyone recently? Maybe you could sketch him for us." Gretchen looks up at Pete as if he's speaking in another language and continues with her sketch.

"Well. You tell him to call his mother as soon as he calls in," Marge is saying as she returns to the kitchen carrying the phone. "You tell him!"

"Patrick must be still out driving Kenny around," Marge says. "If there was ever an excuse for police brutality, Kenny's it. Of course,' she adds shaking her head, "he didn't stand much of a chance with that mother of his."

"Is there anyone in this town whose history you don't know?" Pete asks as she joins them at the table.

"When you've been around as long as I have, you learn quite a lot about people…not all of it good," Marge concludes philosophically.

"Well, I want you to know I appreciate all your help, Marge, especially looking after Willie tonight. This has not been easy for him."

"Do you think he knows?" Marge asks.

"I do. I think he knows much more than he tells," Pete says, turning to look at Willie.

The Dead Woman in His Room

"I wish I'd been able to spend more time with him when I was growing up. He was a jazz musician, you know. He was good, too. Traveled all over the world, playing music. He used to send me postcards. Now that I think about it," Pete adds, "I never saw him perform except with my mom at home. Kind of sad. I wish I knew him better. He's really my only family."

The three of them sit looking over at Willie on the couch. It's hard to imagine him playing his horn on stage in some jazz club in Frankfurt, Germany, or Tokyo or Reno, all the places he has stickers from on his luggage. Where did all those experiences go? Where is he now? Pete wonders.

Gretchen interrupts Pete's reverie by pushing something under his hand on the table. It's a sketch of two men seen through the window of a U-Rent van. One of them is clearly Kenny with his weak chin and big ears. The other man is dark, intense looking. He has a big head with his hair slicked back. "Nick, Nick, Nick," she says.

"Jesus. That must be him," Pete exclaims, jumping up. "Gretchen, I love you." He leans over and hugs her bony shoulders and kisses her on top of her head.

Pete holds up Gretchen's sketch. "Look at this! Gretchen has sketched the killer. It's got to be him."

Ralph and Bud approach the table. "Have either of you seen him around. Sorry Bud," Pete puts his hand on Bud's shoulder. "Have you seen this guy, Ralph?"

Ralph shakes his head; no. Ralph is even quieter than usual. He's more upset by what happened this evening than any of them know. He's ashamed of his inability to intervene. All these people are so engaged in life, and he is so detached. Any one of them would have run in and stopped that awful fight. He knows Bud would. And Bud's blind.

Depression is sucking at Ralph, drawing him down into a pit of self-loathing. He's been self-medicating recently, or more accurately, self-un-medicating by cutting back on his drugs. He wants to feel more alive. Now, in his mind, he is flagellating himself with a long list of his inadequacies that he uses with skillful effect like a whip on his psyche.

"The perogies are ready," Anna announces proudly. A wall of steam rises up around her when she pours the slippery things into a colander in the sink. "Who's hungry?"

Anna's made this batch with onions and garlic and the smell wafts through the apartment. Anna is right. Food does ease the tension in the room. Just back from faxing Gretchen's sketch to her son, Marge starts putting out plates and silverware for everyone. "Bring over those chairs, would you, Pete? We'll crowd around the table."

No one notices Willie leave.

Pete saves a place for Willie at the table but, when he goes over to the couch to get him, he isn't there. He sees that the bathroom door is shut and walks toward it. "Willie, you in there? Anna made perogies. Come on and have some with us," he adds, "You like perogies. Willie? Willie? Are you all right?" Pete taps on the door. "Willie, come on answer me. Are you in there?"

By now everyone is watching Pete at the bathroom door. Pete looks back toward them and holds his palms up in a sign of query. He isn't particularly alarmed, yet. "Willie." He taps again on the door. He tries the doorknob. It's unlocked. "Willie. Come on, Willie, are you in there. Answer me. Finally, he pushes the door open far enough to look around it.

"Damn it." He pushes the door open. "He's not in there. Jesus. He's not here. Did anyone see Willie leave?"

Marge points to her bedroom—the only other room in the apartment.

Pete dashes into the bedroom and comes out as quickly. "He's not there. Willie's gone. We've got to find him. That guy could be out there. Jesus. How could this happen?"

"Pete. We'll find him." Foxy stands up. "He can't have gone far. He was just here. You look on the north stairs. Ralph and I will look on the south stairs. He's probably just gone back to his apartment."

"You're right." Pete says. "We'll meet back here. How far could he get?"

"Let's make sure he didn't go downstairs where he might get out of the building," Foxy says to Ralph. "We can check for him upstairs later." Bud follows Foxy and Ralph down the south stairs.

~~~

Kenny does know the building well. He also has a key to a backdoor that is intended for the staff. It leads into the basement and connects there to a set of interior stairs that come out behind the security desk and continue one flight above that to a mezzanine. There are only two rooms on the mezzanine. One is the director Pam Hart's office. She has her desk situated so she can look down on people as they walk through the foyer. Some residents actually time their comings and goings around when Pam will be off duty. The other room on the mezzanine is crowded with all the controls for the building, including power, communications, and the security system. Murph, the older security guard is the only one who has a key to this room. It's his inner sanctum.

Murph is on duty when Kenny leads Nick upstairs from the basement. It's quiet. The lobby is empty and Murph is getting ready to make his rounds. Security cameras are good, but Murph feels obliged to walk the grounds and see for himself that all is well. He takes security very personally. There are no security cameras on the staff entrance.

Nick appears suddenly beside him and directs him with the point of his knife toward the door to the stairs. Murph can tell by Nick's eyes that resisting him would be pointless. Murph knew people like this one in the Army when he was in Vietnam. He recognizes that hollowness behind his eyes like the guys in long range reconnaissance patrols had when they returned from month-long patrols in the jungles. They exuded death.

"Don't speak," Nick says, slipping Murph's gun out of the holster on his belt and pushing him up the stairs toward the security room. Kenny is at the top of the stairs, looking anxious. Kenny steps aside as Nick pushes Murph across a narrow hallway to the security room door.

"Open it." Murph does as he's told. This is the one room that is equipped with an ID reader. Nick takes Murph's ID card from his hand after he uses it to open the door. Then he shoves him roughly into the room.

The room is lit by the glow from the security monitors. There are no windows. The walls are covered with shelves that hold computer equipment for the building's network system. The wiring closet for the phone system is in one corner and a breaker box for the electrical system is mounted across from it. Security monitors are stacked across the back edge of a utility table against the far wall. There is one chair in the room, an old oak armchair with a dark green pad tied to the seat.

Nick pulls the chair off to one side and pushes Murph down onto it. "I need the pass keys to the rooms. Where are they?"

"Who are you?" Murph barely finishes his question when Nick backhands him across the face.

"No questions. Just answers. The pass keys. Now."

Nick is standing in front of Murph. Kenny has gone over to look at the monitors.

Murph unhooks a key chain from his belt. It has twelve keys on it, one for each floor. They are numbered. The same pass key opens all the doors on one floor. Because most of the residents of the High Rise are elderly and it might become necessary to gain access to their apartments in an emergency, the residents are not allowed to have any other locks for the apartments. Any that are installed are removed. The fact that there are security monitors and a 24-hour security force—Murph, Jeffery and a quiet little

Sicilian guy named Guido who works the late shift—is supposed to be enough to re-assure the residents that they are safe in their apartments. Bonded lock smiths are not allowed in the building, but removing an assortment of hastily installed locks, chains and sliders is an on-going challenge.

Nick seems to be considering what to do with Murph when Kenny holds out a roll of duct tape. He does not want to be an accessory to murder. "Want me to tape him to the chair? I can do it good."

"Yeah sure." Nick is preoccupied. He checks each key to make sure they are all there. Then he looks intently around the room, as if memorizing it.

Murph knows instinctively what Kenny is doing. He does not resist. Kenny is very thorough, taping each ankle to a chair leg, each wrist to a chair arm and several wraps around Murph's torso to hold him against the back. Then he puts a strip of tape across Murph's mouth.

"You did good," Nick says to Kenny. Then he stands in front of Murph, takes his chin in his hand and turns his face up so he can look into his eyes. "This must be your lucky day, asshole," he says before smashing Murph's gun across the side of his forehead. The chair rocks back precariously but lands upright. Murph's head flops down on his chest. Kenny turns away from the bleeding. He really hopes Murph isn't dead…for his own sake. Kenny always makes sure he's on the side of the bully; but this guy is way more than a bully. Kenny is terrified.

"Show me the stairs," Nick says. "You first."

They go back down one flight from the mezzanine to the first floor where they can pick up the main staircase. The closest one to them is on the south side.

17

"Can't talk. He's here!"

Foxy and Ralph catch up with Willie on the basement level. Willie walked downstairs as far as he could go and then became disoriented when there were no more stairs to walk down. Foxy almost missed him in the shadows behind where the stairs enter the basement.

Foxy approaches him gently and takes his hand. "Willie. It's Foxy. Ralph and Bud are here, too. Let's go back upstairs, Willie."

"I want to go home," Willie says. He isn't agitated. He just seems very tired.

"I know you do, Willie," Foxy says. "I know you do. We'll take you there."

They start back up the stairs. Foxy and Willie first, followed by Bud and then Ralph. It's slow going. Willie sets the pace. They've almost reached the third floor.

Ralph is the first to become aware of people catching up to them in the staircase. Surprised to hear people coming upstairs, Ralph turns to see who it is.

Kenny appears first, followed by a much bigger man. As they enter the landing below him, Ralph recognizes Nick from Gretchen's drawing. He turns and stops in the middle of the stairs. Still agonizing over his inability to intervene when Kenny beat up Jen, Ralph is determined to stand his ground this time. He knows Bud would.

"Hey, Kenny. Who's your friend?" He calls out by way of warning Foxy and Bud of their unexpected companions in the staircase.

Hearing his name from above, Kenny stops with his hand on the corner post. Nick comes around behind Kenny and looks up to where the voice came from. He looks past Ralph just in time to see Foxy pushing Willie through the door to the 3rd floor.

Bud shuts the door behind her and leans against it. He has his white cane in front of him moving it back and forth across the edge of the landing.

Nick bounds up the stairs, yanking at the banister for more speed. At the last minute Ralph steps in his way, temporarily knocking Nick off balance so that he twists backwards over the railing. Emboldened by his temporary advantage, Ralph reaches out with both hands and pushes Nick backwards. Ralph, however, has neither the strength nor the heart for combat. Nick easily swings his left arm under Ralph's and flicks him against the wall as if he weighed nothing. Ralph bounces back from the wall directly into Nick's fist which spins him around and carries him several stairs lower before he crashes into the wall and tumbles the rest of the way to the landing where Kenny still stands looking up.

Kenny has seen enough. He runs down the stairs. Ralph just lays there like a big rag doll piled on itself.

Bud steps in front of Nick as he reaches the landing, but Nick shoves him out of the way, grabbing his cane and breaking it in half before darting through the door.

The hallway on the third floor is empty and quiet. Foxy and Willie are hiding in Gladys' apartment. The third door down. Foxy counted on it not being locked. Gladys hasn't locked her door since the day two months ago when she fell, and the fire department had to be called to pick her up off the floor. It took four men.

The Dead Woman in His Room

Nick stops at the beginning of the hall and listens. Then, using the pass key that he took from Murph, he starts opening doors. "Fire marshal," he calls out as he pushes open the first door on the right and rushes into the Rubenthal's apartment.

At that time, Jacob Rubenthal is pacing the floor trying to figure out who and where he is, and his wife, Marie, is staying out of his way. Jacob is in a very aggressive stage of Alzheimer's and has pushed Marie away from him for the first time in their 44 years of marriage.

Having Nick burst in the middle of this scene has almost no impact on the Rubenthal's. Marie watches him poke his head inside every closed door in the apartment and then, as quickly as he entered, rush back into the hall. Jacob takes no notice of the intrusion at all.

~~~

Pete is running up the stairs on the other side of the building when he hears his cell phone ring. He looks at the caller ID. He's breathing hard when he answers it.

"Foxy?"

"Yeah. I can't talk. I have Willie with me. We're safe. Kenny and that guy were in the staircase. I think Ralph is hurt and maybe Bud, too. They're just below the 3rd floor. I think you should call the police."

"Where are you!?"

"Can't talk. He's here!" She hangs up.

~~~

Nick is pushed back by the heat and the smell when he rushes into Gladys' apartment. Although the TV is on, the apartment appears to be empty. There is a Barca-lounger chair in the middle of the room, draped with blankets. Next to it is a portable commode that has been reinforced with steel tubing. It must be 85 degrees in the apartment, and the heat has cooked the smell from the commode with the smell of chlorine and garlic. The result is an imposing wall of odor.

The Dead Woman in His Room

Nick walks into the apartment far enough to see that there is no one in the main room and then turns down the hall to the bathroom. Gladys is standing there, all 450 pounds of her. Actually, she's a little lighter, having decided to get her stomach stapled after her humiliating encounter with the fire department. Gladys is, in fact, very proud of herself for being able to stand on her own for the first time in four months. It is a complete stroke of luck that she was practicing this feat when Foxy and Willie burst into her apartment and told her they needed to hide. Getting to her feet is not something Gladys can rush.

Standing in the hallway to the bathroom, she fills the entire width of the hall up to about five feet. Gladys is aware of the reaction most people have when they see her, especially when they aren't expecting her. "We fat people are the last of the untouchables," Gladys told Foxy one time. "No one wants to touch us."

Nick recoils visibly when he comes around the corner and sees Gladys. "Jesus," he says, making a face and turning away. Then he repeats, "Fire marshal. Have to check the rooms," and moves tentatively toward Gladys.

Gladys doesn't move. She smiles. "I wouldn't go in there right now if I were you, honey," she says, raising a huge arm with a little fat hand on the end of it. She squeezes her nose and winks. "You might want to come back later." When she moves toward him, it looks as if she is being extruded from the hall. Nick is aware of a huge mass of flesh in slow motion.

There is no way he can get around her, and he lets his revulsion convince him that no one else could have either. He turns away and rushes out of the apartment, letting the door slam shut behind him.

Foxy and Willie are crammed together face to face in the small bathroom. Not knowing what else to do, Foxy holds one finger in front of her mouth to signal Willie to be quiet. Whether he understands the gesture or not, he is quiet. Afterwards Foxy begins laughing nervously. To her surprise Willie joins her, and then holds his index finger in front of her mouth and smiles. Willie is definitely still in there somewhere.

~~~

Pete was on his way to the 8th floor. Jamming the cell phone back into his shirt pocket, he hits the fire door running, runs the length of the hall to the south stairwell and dashes down the stairs, taking several steps at a time, catching himself on the banister occasionally to keep from falling headlong down the stairs in his frantic hurry.

He bounces off the wall on the 3rd floor landing and is about to leap down the next flight when he looks down and sees officer Henderson looking up at him from the landing below. Bud is standing with his back to the wall, and Henderson is kneeling over Ralph, feeling for a pulse. He looks up when he hears Pete above him.

"You!" Henderson yells. "I knew it. Stop right there. You're under arrest."

Henderson is on his own. Petruzio got a call shortly after leaving Willie's apartment that his wife Maureen was in the hospital. She had a heart attack in one of her patient's homes. As he jumped out of the car in front of the emergency room, Petruzio shouted back at Henderson, "Don't do anything stupid, okay. Just don't do anything at all until I get back."

Henderson spent the intervening time convincing himself that Pete killed the woman on River Street, and that he should arrest him before he killed again. It would be his collar, not Petruzio's. Petruzio is dragging his feet on this. He's too old and fat to be a cop anymore. He's lost his edge. Henderson has his edge. He should make the arrest. In the end, his circular logic convinces him that Pete is guilty, that Petruzio is incompetent and that he, officer Henderson, is about to realize every cop's dream and become a legend in his own time. Henderson is having an epiphany.

Now here's Pete with what looks like another dead body. Henderson charges up the stairs at Pete, drawing his gun from his shoulder holster as he goes. "You're under arrest."

Already stunned by the image of Ralph lying unconscious on the landing with Bud kneeling next to him, Pete hesitates as Henderson charges at him with his gun in his outstretched hand. He knows he needs to get to Foxy and Willie, and that need directs his kick. He connects with Henderson's hand and the impact knocks the gun free and sends it spinning across the stairwell. It also throws Henderson off balance. His momentum carries him further up the stairs, but the kick to his right hand has twisted him around backwards. Pete plants his foot between Henderson's shoulder blades and pushes. Henderson dives down the stairs landing hard, face down, just two steps above Ralph. Pete is out of the stairs and running down the hall before Henderson slides the rest of the way to the landing.

18

"I've got your bitch!"

Marge is pacing. Though it has often been her role, she doesn't like waiting while the action takes place elsewhere. She has the police scanner on, but there is nothing coming across. She already faxed the picture Gretchen drew to her son at the police station. Why weren't they responding? She hates not knowing what is happening. It is taking much too long for them to find Willie and bring him back. The killer is out there. She's sure of it. The killer is out there with people she has come to care very much about. She has to do something.

Reasoning that more confusion would be better in these circumstances, Marge sends Anna into the hall to set off the fire alarm. It's not an easy thing for Anna to do, but, after struggling with her extreme reluctance to break anything, Anna smashes the glass with the ax and pulls the chain. She actually finds the experience exciting and brings the ax back to Marge's apartment triumphantly as the fire alarm begins howling throughout the building.

Confusion is accomplished. Besides the old people struggling out of their apartments on canes, walkers and scooters, the sounds of their television sets blast into the hallway each time another door opens. Many High Rise residents can't hear very well so their televisions are often turned up loud. The bubbly sounds of Lawrence Welk blast into the hall when frail Mrs.

The Dead Woman in His Room

Lipinski urges her walker out the door blending uncomfortably with the monotone chant of a Catholic mass from the Brancini's. The sounds of machine guns and dive bombers accompany the elder Mr. Ekman into the hall. He plays World War II documentaries on his television constantly. Different versions of the afternoon TV cacophony blast into the hallways on every floor of the High Rise as the fire alarm drives the residents out of their apartments.

~~~

Anxious to get Willie back up to Marge's apartment, Foxy has Willie by the hand and is rushing for the stairwell when Nick emerges from the Yoplanski's apartment. It has to be Nick. Gretchen definitely captured the sense of him in her sketch. Nick recognizes Willie immediately and starts toward them in a straight line, pushing people out of his way. He moves through the people as if he is walking through tall grass. He has his arms raised. He points at Foxy and mouths "Stop." Then he holds his right hand out like a gun, and he pantomimes shooting at the people in the hall. He mouths "Stop" again.

Foxy stops. They are right in front of the elevator. She pulls Willie behind her protectively. As Nick approaches, the elevator doors open and some of the more alert elderly push past them into the elevator. At the last second, before Nick reaches them, Foxy butts Willie backwards into the elevator and stands in front of the door as it closes. Nick comes up very close, but he is too late. Willie, at least, is gone.

Nick grabs Foxy's arm and shoves her into a recently vacated apartment across the hall. He slams the door shut and pins her against it with his body.

~~~

Pete is working his way up the floors trying to find Foxy and Willie. He races up the stairs, rushes the length of the hall and then runs up the opposite stairwell to the next floor. All the people in the hallways are slowing him down. Many of them recognize him and want to talk. Pete always stops to talk. But this time he doesn't.

His cell phone rings. He holds it in front of him to look at the Caller ID. It's Foxy's number.

"I've got your bitch in room 307," he hears Nick say. "Bring Willie and meet me here. No tricks or she dies."

"I don't have Willie."

"Get him."

Nick hangs up.

Foxy said Willie was with her. Pete was sure of it. Or had been. How could this guy have Foxy and not Willie? Maybe he's lying. But he did have Foxy's cell phone, so he must have Foxy.

As Pete stands processing the implications of his call from Nick, Bud shows up beside him.

"He's got Foxy," Pete says. "But Willie is missing. I've got to find him."

"We'll find him," Bud says. "If I find him, I'll take him to Marge's."

"Good. How's Ralph?"

"I don't know."

"Good luck," Pete says as Bud sets off, extending his broken cane in the air in front of him as if he's dueling with an imaginary assailant.

~~~

Chaos escalates as more old people pour into the hallways and jam the elevators; some of them are terrified at the thought of being caught in a burning building, others don't know where they are or why.

Pete is momentarily stopped. Then he remembers the letter Willie gave him earlier that evening—could it only have been that evening.

"That's it." He pulls the letter out of his back pocket where he had stuffed it after reading it in Willie's apartment. He must be after the funds that were deposited in HAL Holdings. He must need the codes. Then he remembers a name: Nick Barons. Willie had called someone Nick Barons. This couldn't be the Nick Barons from the letter. It must be someone who looks like Nick Barons.

Pete calls Foxy's cell phone.

"I know who you are," Pete says as soon as he hears the call being answered. "You're Nick Barons' son, aren't you?" Pete waits for what seems like a very long time. "I have the codes for HAL Holdings."

"Well. Aren't you smart." Pete hears Nick say finally. "I have the girl."

"I'm willing to trade. Are you?"

"Maybe."

"Meet me in the hallway on the fourth floor in front of the elevators."

"No. We meet here in 307."

"You want the codes? You and Foxy, fourth floor, three minutes." Pete hangs up. It's a huge bluff. He knows he'll have nothing left to bargain with if he gives him the codes. He'll kill them both. At least in the hall, he and Foxy have a chance. He's making this up as he goes.

Pete rushes to the hallway on the fourth floor, wishing he had said two minutes instead of three. Time is going slow. The fire alarm is still going off and Pete hears sirens outside in the parking lot.

Nick is as impatient at Pete. The fire alarm in the hallways and the sirens outside the building all remind him of a prison riot in LA that happened not too long after he was sent up for assault the first time. That experience was one of the reasons he hated being in tall buildings like the High Rise. He feels trapped. His need to get out threatens to overwhelm all other thoughts.

This guy Pete said he has the codes. He hangs on to that thought. That's all he needs. He also hangs on to Foxy. She has balls. He'll give her that. She's a cool one. He feels the strength in her, and it arouses him. No time for that now.

"Let's go," he says, jerking Foxy around to face him and pressing up against her. "That's a gun in my pocket and if you do anything stupid, I'll shoot your friend first. Understood."

Foxy nods her head.

"For you I have a knife," he says. Then he spins her around by twisting her arm painfully in front of him. He presses her hard against the door with his whole body for a moment and then reaches beside her to turn the knob with his left hand.

~~~

The scene is total chaos. The hallways are filled with old people, some of them with walkers, some with scooters; some are frightened, some are enjoying the excitement, some wander aimlessly against the tide of the more coherent residents milling around in front of the elevators. The fire alarm continues to howl, and a red light spins insistently over the exit doors to the stairs at each end of the hall. None of these people can take the stairs. Without the elevators. They're all trapped.

Nick looks down the hall and sees Pete in the center of the action in front of the elevators. Pete's looking over his way, but an old lady who clutches a shawl around her with one hand is jerking on Pete's sleeve with the other.

"No, this isn't Bingo night, Mrs. P. This is Sunday night," Pete says leaning down to her level. "Bingo is Wednesday night." Then he adds, "I'm a little busy right now. I'm meeting someone."

Pushing Foxy ahead of him, Nick makes his way down the hall toward Pete. It's not easy going. Several of the elderly residents look automatically to them for assistance, just because they are younger. Most of them know Foxy and expect her to speak with them the way she always does. They look askance at the big dark man behind her who is pushing her past them down the hall. Their cognition may be compromised, but they sense the violence in this man.

The Dead Woman in His Room

"Are we going to be all right, Foxy? Will we die in the fire?"

"It's not a fire, Lilly. Don't worry. It's a false alarm. You'll be all right." Foxy says as she is pushed past a grey-haired woman stooped over a walker. "Don't be afraid."

Nick jerks Foxy back in front of him. "Be afraid, bitch," he snarls into the back of her head. "Be very afraid."

They are close now. Pete can see the blue in Foxy's eyes.

"Let her go," Pete says to the brown eyes looking over Foxy's head. "I've got what you want."

Nick twists Foxy's arm up tighter behind her back. She winces in pain. Nick sees the elevator light come on. He plans to push Foxy into Pete and ram them both into the elevator when the doors open. He's sure it'll be empty. No one would be coming up into this nut house. Everyone wants to go down.

The elevator dings and the doors open, but just before he surges ahead, Nick sees two men in the elevator. One is in a cop uniform.

"That's him," the other one says. "Grab him." The cop reaches out and grabs Pete's upraised arm and jerks him into the elevator. Pete twists his head around in amazement.

The other man is officer Henderson. "Remember me," he says to Pete.

Just as the doors start to close, Nick shoves Foxy hard, almost lifting her off her feet and throwing her into the elevator ahead of him. Foxy slams into Pete and he, in turn, knocks the two cops against the back wall.

The elevator doors close.

Nick hits the stop button and pulls Murph's gun from his jacket pocket. It is suddenly quiet. Time stops. It's a small elevator, made even smaller by the padding that was hung on the walls to protect it from the constant moving of furniture in and out of the High Rise as people die or move into nursing homes and new old people take their place.

The Dead Woman in His Room

This is Foxy's nightmare. Not the guy with the gun, and the knife. Not his very real threat to their lives. The elevator. Foxy is terrified of elevators. She begins to gulp for air. Panic overwhelms her as the fear of her fear cascades through her nervous system. Without saying a word, she drops senseless to the floor.

Foxy's fall startles everyone. Including Nick. He backs into the corner in front of the control panel. Pete drops to his knees next to Foxy and pulls her into his arms. He expects to see blood. The cop in uniform and the other guy flatten against the back wall, staring at the gun in Nick's hand.

"What the…" the cop says, looking up from the gun to Nick's face. "This man is under arrest. Who the hell are you?"

"I'm the one with the gun," Nick says. "That's all you need to know. This man has something of mine, and I'm here to collect it. You can have him when I'm done."

"But…" Henderson starts to say.

"But nothing, asshole." Nick raises the gun until it is pointed directly into Henderson's face. "Understand?" He pushes the gun under Henderson's chin. "Say yes."

"Yes."

"That's better." Nick looks down at Pete where he crouches on the floor over Foxy.

"The codes. We had a deal, remember." He points the gun at Foxy. "I can still take her back."

"I'll give you the codes," Pete says looking up at Nick. "You're the one who killed Candice, aren't you?"

"I don't know any Candice. Just give me the fucking codes." He reaches out his hand. "The codes."

"You're not going to get away with this," Henderson speaks from the back of the elevator, interrupting Nick's focus on Pete.

"You," Nick turns to Henderson. "Didn't I tell you to shut up."

"There are cops all around this building," Henderson says. "You'll never get out of here."

The Dead Woman in His Room

"They're looking for him, not me. They can have him." Nick pauses a moment, thinking. "Actually, I think we'll all leave together." Nick steps aside and flips the elevator back on. Looking at Henderson he says, "We'll take your car." He pushes the button for the basement.

"You…with the uniform. Stand in front of this door and don't let anyone on. Tell them it's police business. Anyone gets on and I'll shoot everyone. But I'll shoot you first. Understood?"

"Yes, sir," The uniformed cop says. He's very scared.

The elevator stops at every floor and each time it stops people try to push their way on and the cop has to hold them off. By the time they get to the basement, the tension seems to suck the air out of the elevator. Foxy is coming to. As the doors open, the uniformed cop crouches to block people, as he has done on all the floors coming down to this one. But when the door opens, instead of holding off a wall of old people, there is no one there.

They all pause, looking out. Then, to everyone's surprise, the uniformed cop sprints out of the elevator and out of sight.

"What the…?" Nick stands in the door with his gun out, looking across the basement after the sound of running footsteps.

~~~

Willie is in the other elevator. He's been riding the elevator up and down since Foxy butted him backwards into it. He stands in the back, politely out of the way. No one notices that when everyone else pours out of the elevator, he does not. He just stands there. When the elevator doors open in the basement, he starts forward, but then steps back and lets the doors close. He doesn't recognize the basement. Actually, he hasn't recognized any of the floors. He doesn't know he's in an elevator. He doesn't know who the hell he is or what he's doing. And he knows enough to know he doesn't. Some part of him stands in the elevator and tries to figure out who he is, but he doesn't have a clue. And the elevator goes up and down with Willie inside trying desperately to find Willie.

In the stairwells and hallways, Bud moves quickly, waving his broken cane in front of him. "Willie," he calls out. "Are you there?" He wants Willie to be able to hear him, but he doesn't know who else might be watching him.

"Willie," he calls over and over again. "Are you there?" People keep bumping into him. It's hard for him to keep his bearings. But he persists, always managing to find his way. Bud always persists. He's worked his way almost to the basement.

Bud's search becomes sighted when Slate catches up with him. Marge had sent Slate out to look for Willie and report back to her. He takes Bud's hand and now they search together.

~~~

Whether it was a stroke of genius or cowardice, the abrupt departure of the uniformed cop has left everyone in the elevator temporarily flummoxed. Pete helps Foxy to her feet.

"Are you all right?"

"Panic disorder," Foxy says. "Elevators." She tips her head back. "Hate elevators."

"Nick is here with us," Pete says, indicating him with his head. "And Henderson. He came to arrest me."

Foxy looks over at Henderson. She is taken aback by his disheveled appearance. There is dried blood on one of his cheeks and the buttons were ripped off his shirt when he slid down the stairs. He is standing there with his mouth open. "What happened to him?"

"He fell down some stairs."

"Oh."

"Okay, folks. There's been a change of plans." Nick steps back inside the elevator and pushes the button for the mezzanine. As the doors shut, they all hear the sound of people running into the basement. Someone shouts, "In there." Foxy clutches Pete involuntarily as the elevator lurches upwards. Henderson staggers forward.

Tossing the gun to his left hand, Nick lets out a howl of frustration and anger and swings his right fist into Henderson's face. Henderson is thrown up against the wall. He seems to hang there suspended for a moment before dropping unconscious to the floor.

"That just leaves us," Nick says, turning to Pete and Foxy as the elevator continues to rise.

~~~

Leaving Henderson behind in the elevator, Nick directs Pete and Foxy back to the security room. He uses Murph's ID to open the door. Then he shoves Pete and Foxy ahead of him, flicks on the light and backs against the door to slam it shut.

Murph is conscious now, tied into the chair where Nick and Kenny left him with the duct tape still tight across his mouth. Murph's pupils are dilated from sitting in the dark and he blinks repeatedly. The blood has dried from the cut on his head where Nick hit him. Nick pushes Pete and Foxy in the corner behind Murph.

"I want to turn off all the lights. Everything." Nick says to Murph. "How do I do that? Show me."

Murph mutters and shakes his head.

Nick yanks the tape from his mouth roughly. "Show me."

"You can't shut off the exit signs. They're on batteries. They go on automatically when it gets dark."

"Fuck the exit signs, what about everything else...wait a minute," Nick is looking into the panel of monitors showing the outside of the building as well as the elevators and the hallways on each. "Let's see who's here first."

The parking lot in front of the High Rise looks like a street riot. There are several police cars, the huge hook and ladder truck from the Mill River fire department and several smaller fire trucks, each with its headlights on and its warning lights flashing. Captured in black and white by the security cameras, the flashing lights give the scene a strobe effect that makes the cops and the firemen milling around between their vehicles appear to jerk across the screen. Closer to the High Rise there is a growing crowd of residents huddled together around their walkers and scooters looking up anxiously toward the High Rise. There appears to be very little contact between the two groups.

"I'm right, aren't I? You're Nick Barons' son," Pete says, interrupting Nick's study of the monitors. "You're too young to have been involved with HAL Holdings."

"Let's just say that the money that should have gone to my mother, my sister and me went into your bank, and never came out."

"It's not my bank," Pete says. "And, besides, the money is still there."

"Yeah. Well, my mother and sister aren't."

"Where are they?"

Nick turns away from the monitors. "They're dead, asshole. Which is what you're going be if you don't shut up."

"I'm just trying to understand."

"Understand this: I only need one of you for a hostage. Which reminds me. I'll take those codes now." He holds out his hand.

When Pete hesitates, Nick pulls the gun out of his belt and aims it at Foxy.

"The codes."

Pete put his hands by his side and stands in front of Foxy. "Kill her and I will not help you."

"Very noble, but I don't need your help. All I need are the codes. I can kill you both and take them right now."

Pete doesn't move. "I *am* the codes," he says.

Nick is thrown off by Pete's statement. "What are you talking about? Where's the paper you showed me? I saw it in your hand."

"That was just a piece of paper. All the codes are in here," Pete points to his head. "Everything you ever wanted to know about HAL Holdings."

Nick looks at Pete in disbelief. He looks back at the monitors; and then back at Pete.

"There's a simple solution to this." Pete says.

"And that is."

"Get me to a computer and I can transfer your money wherever you want it."

"There's a computer," Nick pointed to the keyboard on the desk.

"No way. We have to get out of here first or no deal," Pete says. "And we have to go somewhere else. I'm not stupid. Once I transfer the money, you don't need me anymore. I'm not doing that here, like this."

"Where then?"

Pete looks aside for a moment, thinking. When he turns back, he's smiling.

"The library."

"What?"

"The public library. They've got computers. I can transfer the money there. You get your money, and you can't shoot me in front of all those avid readers."

"You've got it all figured out, don't you? You think you're real smart."

"You got a better idea?" Pete thinks maybe he was getting too far into the role with that last comment. He knows he's toying with a bull. He doesn't want to piss him off too much.

"Turn around," Nick says abruptly. "Turn around," he indicates with his gun. Pete has the horrible feeling Nick is going to kill him right then. But, when Pete turns around, Nick reaches in both of his back pockets.

"Look at me, now. Empty your front pockets. Pull 'em out."

The Dead Woman in His Room

Pete does as he's told. He pulls out a small wallet and a set of keys. "Nothing up my sleeve," he says pulling up his sleeves. He's hoping Nick won't see where he stuck Candice's letter in the rack of manuals for the security system while Nick was occupied with the security monitors.

"You better be right or I'm going to kill you twice," Nick says, pointing the gun, first at Foxy and then at Pete. "You better be right."

"Leave her here. She doesn't know anything about any of this." Pete looks around him. "Where's the tape you used on him? I'll do it myself."

"Nah," Nick says. "She's coming too. Anything goes wrong at any point. I'll kill her first. You may be the codes, but she's my insurance. They won't take any of us alive. I promise you that." Nick motions to Pete and Foxy to come around in front of him.

"You first," he says. "We'll go out the way I came in."

19

"I killed them with a knife so I could watch them die."

Petruzio was in the emergency room with his wife Maureen when Henderson was wheeled in. Henderson's jaw was badly broken, and he couldn't talk. He didn't need to.

"You went to arrest Rangely, didn't you?" Petruzio says leaning over Henderson on the stretcher.

Henderson nods his head.

"He didn't do this, did he?"

Henderson nods again.

"Damn it. I knew there was someone else. I knew it." He pounds on the railing around Henderson's gurney. "I'll deal with you later," he says, turning away.

From their beds in the emergency room, with very different emotions, Henderson and Petruzio's wife Maureen, both watch him rush out the door.

At this point, the fire department knows it's a false alarm, but they also know from the police that there is at least one armed and dangerous person in the building and there might be a hostage situation. Petruzio tells Lt. Brunoli, the ranking fire fighter on the scene, to keep the people outside as long as he can. Then he coordinates a search of the building with a few cops, ones he knows personally. Marge's son Patrick is among them. He shows Petruzio the fax his mother had sent. It was relayed from the police station to his patrol car.

"This may be the guy, we're looking for." He tells Petruzio.

"Where the hell did this come from?" Petruzio wants to know.

"My mother. One of her friends drew this. Seems this one," he says, pointing to Nick, "has been paying this other guy, Kenny, a druggie who lives in the High Rise, to spy on Rangely and his uncle. She found out from Kenny's wife, after Kenny beat her up. It's a long story."

"Sounds like it," Petruzio says. "We should put your mother on the police force."

"She thinks she already is," Patrick says.

"Yeah. I know Marge. She wouldn't be the worst cop we have. Pretty good sketch, too."

"You won't believe who did that."

"Don't tell me. Enough of this is hard to believe. Listen, I want you and Roxanne to start a search of the building. Go up the south stairwell and check each floor as you go. I've got Hagstrum and Mancini going up the north stairwell. Is there any other way out of the building besides these main doors?" Petruzio asks.

"I don't think so. Hey, did you talk to Murph, the security guy? He's been here since this place was built. He knows everything about it. This place is his life." Patrick adds, "If he's not here, something else is wrong. Did anyone check the utility room where the computers that run the security cameras are kept? That's like Murph's second home. You can see the whole building from that room. Actually, you could run the whole building from that room. All the controls are there."

"Show me."

Suddenly the lights go off in the whole building. Everything but the exit lights. A gasp rises up from the crowd.

"That's where they are," Patrick yells. They start running toward the building.

~~~

The Dead Woman in His Room

It's eerily quiet inside the High Rise. The red glow from the exit signs gives it the appearance of a giant photographer's dark room. Everything appears in shades of red. Darkness pools up in the corners.

Nick is planning to take advantage of the confusion caused by abruptly turning off all the lights to conceal their escape. It's a good plan. There is a gap in the attention of the police and firemen. The firemen at this point have become occupied with their equipment and each other. The police are occupied with crowd control. Some of them have parents or other relatives in the crowd and seeing them while they are on duty makes it seem like a big open house. When the lights in the High Rise go out, many of the residents become alarmed and push in among the fire trucks and police cars to get away from the brooding darkness of the High Rise. The attention of the police is focused on the crowd, not the exits.

Nick is headed for the staff door in the basement. It would be especially dark there.

~~~

Willie was lost in the elevator. He saw people coming and going. He heard some of them talk. He saw the lights blink and smelled the people and felt it when someone pressed against him or accidentally hit him with an elbow or a cane or a walker. All the stimuli are recorded by his eyes and ears and nose and skin, but the messages with the sights and sounds and smells and touch stop short of where he is in his mind.

He is aware of being in his body, but he can no longer make it do anything. He is aware of the eye holes in his skull that he sees through, but he can't process what he sees. He feels very clear in his mind, but he feels as if he is only mind. His body is as separate from him as the walls of the elevator. He's ridden the elevator up and down several times.

The Dead Woman in His Room

Bud and Slate make it to the basement just as the elevator doors slide open. When Slate looks inside, he sees Willie standing in the back.

Their reunion is rushed. Knowing that the person who wants to hurt Willie is inside the building, Bud is determined to get Willie outside the building. Though he can't see, he knows the building well. His years below decks on ships made staying oriented second nature. He explored every inch of the High Rise and the map in his mind is almost an exact replica of the building schematics. He also knows they are in the basement by the smell of it.

Bud tells Slate to stand in the doorway and keep the doors open while he tries to talk Willie into getting off the elevator with them. Bud can't see Willie's body, but he is aware of him, and the Willie he is aware of is the one inside Willie. A sighted person may have been distracted by Willie's body standing there unmoving. Bud is aware of Willie's presence. He can almost reach him there. But not quite.

Bud doesn't notice when the lights go out. But Slate does. An instant wave of darkness seems to push him into the elevator.

"The lights went out, Bud," Slate says. "I can't see. What should I do?"

"Stay close to me, Slate. It's all right. I know how to get around in the dark. Help me get Willie. I'm going to carry him out on my back. I need you to hold his arms up over my shoulders so I can grab them." Bud backs into Willie and Slate helps him get hold of Willie's arms. "Okay, Slate. I'll do the rest."

Bud staggers out of the elevator with Willie draped on his back just as Foxy and Pete step into the basement from the back stairs. Nick is close behind them. He has Murph's gun in his hand.

They all become aware of each other at the same time and stop. All the lights are out except the exit signs. They look at each other across the darkened basement. Bud sways from side to side as if adjusting his internal radar to the new surroundings and the people in it. He lets Willie slide off his back, and he reaches out and takes his broken cane from Slate's hand. Willie stands on his own. Slate steps behind Bud.

"Well, well, well," Nick breaks the silence. "Look who we have here. Too bad we don't have time to chat." Nick pokes Pete's back with the gun. Pete keeps Foxy in front of him, so he is between her and Nick.

When Bud takes his hand, Willie finds he can move. He takes a step. When Nick's voice reaches him from across the basement, he finds he can hear. When he looks toward the sound, he finds he can see.

Then he finds he can speak.

"Nick Barons," Willie says. "You're Nick Barons, aren't you?"

Being recognized stops Nick, briefly. He is never recognized, certainly not by that name. He recognizes Willie and the blind guy. He remembers shoving him out of his way on the stairs and breaking his cane. Bud is irrelevant to Nick.

"Is Kyle with you?" Willie asks. "I haven't seen Kyle lately." He approaches Nick. And Bud comes with him. "Where's Kyle?"

Kyle is a name that Nick pursued like the holy grail for three years. It was the strongest living link to his father, and it was so associated with his hatred for his father that just hearing it spoken squirts adrenaline through his system. Having spoken it, Willie becomes the last living thing associated with that name. Willie knew his father. Nick stops and looks at Willie, approaching him in the red twilight from the exit signs.

"Your friend Kyle is dead," Nick says. "I killed him myself. The broad, Constance. I killed her, too." He looks for his statement to hurt Willie. He wants to hurt Willie, but Willie doesn't understand. "Constance. Kyle and Constance. I killed them both. I killed them with a knife so I could watch them die."

Willie keeps coming closer. Shuffling. Peering into the shadows. He isn't getting it. "Aren't you Nick Barons? I knew Nick Barons. Are you Nick Barons?"

The Dead Woman in His Room

Willie is closer now. Bud is with him, but Nick only sees Willie. "Nick," Willie says. "Where's Kyle, Nick? Is he with you?"

Time seems suspended. Pete and Foxy watch in slow motion as Willie approaches Nick. It's like watching an unknowing child approach a bull in the field. "Is Kyle with you? I'd like to see Kyle again," Willie says.

Nick still has the gun in his right hand. He shifts it to his left and reaches in his pocket. He couldn't kill Willie before. But now he can. This guy knew his father. This guy helped his father steal everything from him and his mother and sister. This guy is going to die. He's walking right into it. He's almost close enough.

This moment for Nick—the moment right before he kills someone—is like the needle prick for a junkie. It is exquisite. He is aware of nothing else.

A commotion from above disrupts the moment. Petruzio and Patrick are coming down the back stairs that Nick used. The sound of their clambering down the stairs from the second floor reaches the basement well ahead of them. It gets louder as they get closer.

Nick looks toward the noise and then toward the back exit, as if judging the time and distance. Willie is close now. Leaning forward to look inquisitively into Nick's face. "Aren't you Nick Barons?" He repeats. "Is Kyle with you?"

Bud hears the click of the knife blade opening. He knows that sound.

Nick is looking into Willie's face. He wants to see his eyes.

The broken tip of Bud's cane catches Nick completely by surprise. It enters just below his ribs, driven forward by the considerable force of both of Bud's hands. Nick tightens his muscles in shock as the cane penetrates, causing him to lean forward slightly just as Bud shifts his stance and pulls up hard with his right hand while his left hand rams the point of the cane almost straight up. Nick slashes out with his knife, but he's too close and there is no strength left in his arm. He sees his own face briefly in a reflection in Bud's dark glasses. Then he drops to the floor with the cane still inside him; Murph's gun still in his left hand, unfired.

Patrick and Petruzio burst into the room in time to see everyone standing in place, staring at Nick crumpled on the floor. The red light from the exit signs makes the blood look black as it spreads like a shadow around his form on the floor.

20

"We're family."

When Pete retrieves Willie's mail from the High Rise post office the next day, there is an official looking letter from the director's office. It's post-marked two days before. Pete opens it as he walks to the elevator. He assumes it's the usual administrative trivia. In fact, the letter is a preliminary notice that Willie is being evicted from the High Rise on the grounds that he is no longer capable of living independently. He is given one month to find a more suitable facility.

The letter is signed, "Regretfully, Pam Hart, executive director."

Pete is crossing in front of the security desk when he reads the signature. Without thinking, he looks up in time to see Pam quickly move away from her window overlooking the foyer. He stands there for a while, looking up. Not even Pam is good enough to be responsible for the timing of this new crisis. He can imagine her fondling the folders in her desk drawer. "The caring bureaucrat." Right.

Pete laughs. He is overloaded. In the scheme of things, this is just one more item on a long list of items to deal with. At least he's been cleared of the murder of the woman he'd found in his room. The woman he now knows as Candice.

Lt. Petruzio came close to apologizing to Pete when he told him that he was "no longer a suspect." He hadn't expected even that much, but Petruzio seemed uncharacteristically forthcoming.

"Hey, after your visit that night, I was beginning to suspect me, too," Pete says. "I'm just glad no one else got hurt."

They are standing together on the steps outside the Mill River Police Station. Petruzio walked Pete outside after their meeting earlier that morning. It is another unusually warm day for September. They closed the file on the murder, but Pete has the impression there is something Petruzio wants to tell him that he doesn't want to say inside.

"How's Henderson, anyway?" Pete asks.

Petruzio laughs. "He can't talk, which is good. But he's going to be all right. Maybe he even learned something."

"They going to give you another partner?"

"I'm retiring," Petruzio says, looking over his glasses at Pete.

"No kidding?"

"Yup. Twenty-eight years is long enough. I'm tired."

"I bet. How's Maureen, by the way? Foxy told me she had a heart attack in a patient's home."

"Maureen's going to be all right. Thanks for asking. We're both going to retire." This is more personal information than Petruzio usually volunteers in a month.

"That's great. What are you two going to do?"

"I'm going to plant my garden." Petruzio seems to surprise himself with his answer. It's a pleasant surprise, at least. "Maureen is thinking about taking in some boarders, elderly people, you know, like her patients. People who need some care but are still active. Kinda like me," he laughs.

"Sounds like a plan. I might even have a boarder for you. Willie can't live on his own in the High Rise, and they won't let me live there with him. I don't honestly know what I'm going to do."

"It's tough. I know. Some of the stories I hear from Maureen make you want to never grow old."

"Beats the alternative. Isn't that what they say?"
"Yeah," Petruzio says. "I guess." They look at each other.

~~~

The details of HAL Holdings never come out in the investigation. The police had a dead woman, and now they have a dead murderer who is implicated in several other investigations. That's enough for them. HAL Holdings, with all its millions, is something else Pete is going to have to figure out what to do with. The only one who knows the whole story is Foxy. It hasn't seemed that important to either of them in the scheme of things. There would be time to deal with HAL Holdings. A more pressing issue is dealing with each other. The intensity of the last 24 hours catapulted their relationship ahead of them, and now they are going to have to figure out what that means. They aren't either of them sure. And they haven't had much time to think about it, much less act on it.

~~~

Bud is with Willie when Pete gets back to his apartment. They're listening to music together. Willie seems relaxed. They both do. Looking at them sitting on the couch listening to music together makes the memory of last night seem like a dream. It's hard to imagine that little more than 12 hours ago Willie stood face to face with a man intent on killing him; harder still to imagine that the blind man next to him saved Willie by ramming the broken end of his cane into the other man's heart. Willie smiles inquisitively when Pete enters the room.

Bud nods his head. "How'd it go downtown?"

"It went okay. Everything is fine, really. I spoke with Petruzio for a while. He said he's retiring; he and Maureen both."

"They going to move in here with us?"

Pete laughs. "No. Actually, they're thinking about converting their house so they can take in some boarders, elderly people, you know, who might need a little more care than they get here."

Bud nods his head toward Willie.

"Maybe."

Bud makes a face as if considering the idea.

"You going to see Ralph?" Pete asks.

"Yeah. I thought I'd go in a little bit."

"Where's Ralph?" Willie asks, sitting up straight. "Has he gone to Bolivia? I think he said something to me about Bolivia. I don't know why he'd want to go there. Where is Bolivia?"

"It's in South America, Willie. Between Brazil and Peru." Pete looks at Bud who seems to feel the look. His dark glasses move up and down in a wink. "Ralph's not in Bolivia, Willie. He's in the hospital for a little while. He's okay, though. He's going to be okay."

"Oh. I hope so." Willie says. "I don't like hospitals."

"Me, either Willie. Me either."

"That's good," Willie says, nodding his head and looking up. "That's good, isn't it?"

"Yeah. That's good, Willie. That's good." Pete takes a deep breath.

Bud stands up at that point. They have a mutual understanding to try not to make it obvious when one of them is spelling the other. Willie sometimes gets angry if he thinks he's being treated as if he needs supervision. It doesn't happen as much as it did just a month before; which isn't necessarily a good sign as far as Willie's cognition is concerned. Things are starting to blur together for Willie. He doesn't notice the changes so much anymore. His short term memory is failing. It's impossible to say what the last 24 hours did to his mind.

Pete follows Bud to the door. It still amazes him how Bud is able to move around as if he can see where he's going. He doesn't take out his new cane until he's standing in the hallway. It's a telescoping cane and it clicks as he extends it. "I think I liked the wood one better," Bud says. "This thing's too light." He taps the floor and moves the cane around experimentally.

"Foxy is coming over later and then Marge said she could stay for a while this evening. I'm staying on the couch. I just don't want to leave him alone, right now."

Bud turns to face Pete. "You can't keep this up forever, Pete."

"I know."

"What are you going to do?"

"I don't know, frankly. I wish I did."

"Well. I'm his friend," Bud says. "You just let me know what I can do, and I'll be here."

"Count on it, man." Pete says. "Count on it." He squeezes Bud's shoulder. "You are a good friend to have. The best."

Bud straightens his back, squares his shoulders, and sets off down the hall at his usual quick pace. Pete watches him walk away.

"What do you want for dinner tonight?" Pete says, walking back into the apartment. "Pizza or Chinese? Your choice. It's all just a phone call away."

Willie smiles. "You're Pete."

"Yup. And you're Willie." Pete sits next to Willie on the sofa. "We're family."

About the author

For characters and a sense of conflict and drama, Mark draws on his decades-long career as a feature writer and magazine editor, his personal experience as a father, son, husband, ex-husband, friend, and lover, as well as his checkered past as a truck driver, land surveyor, tree surgeon, ditch digger, lead guitarist, and hitchhiker around the world on freelance story assignments. Mark and his wife live in a little red house in an old mill town in New England.

Books by the author

The Mill River Series

Book 1: *The Dead Woman in His Room*

> Pete Rangely came to Mill River to care for his uncle who is suffering from Alzheimer's. When he finds a dead woman in his hotel room, he assumes she has nothing to do with him or his uncle. He's wrong.

Book 2: *Hospice for Murder*

> When Foxy McFarlane finds a dead girl on the mountain, it tears a hole in the tangled web of devotion and deceit that conceals sex-trafficking, medical malpractice, and murder behind a curtain of true believers at the Doorways to Heaven Church in a blue-collar New England town.

Made in United States
North Haven, CT
14 January 2025